A Narrow Road

Pulling Back the Curtains of Heaven
Breaking through the darkness
A collection of short stories

A NARROW ROAD

Pulling back the curtains of heaven
Breaking through the darkness
A collection of short stories
© 2001 By: David B. Rossman

ABE CLARY CREATIVE PORTRAITS
301 Yelm Ave E Yelm, WA 98597

DAVID B. ROSSMAN
P.O. Box 2072 Yelm, WA 98597-2072

Email: lordspoet@hotmail.com

Or visit my website
http://www.members.tripod.com/~PoetrybyDavid

Library of Congress Control Number: 2002090284
ISBN: 0-9718475-0-9

Printed in the United States by:
Morris Publishing
3212 East Highway 30
Kearney, NE 68847
1-800-650-7888

FOREWORD

By Dan Wooding

Through the window we watch the winds of life change before our eyes. From second to second, moment to moment, emotions switch.

How often do we catch a glimpse of what is important to us? Do we even listen to what we hear? Can we comprehend the meaning of what we are told?

Within these pages of David Rossman's latest book, the Spirit flows to show the love of God, affecting lives throughout the nations through opening the heart of one man.

We may sing and dance, fret and weep, but there's one thing that can lead us down the right path...that being A NARROW ROAD.

Dan Wooding is the Founder and President of ASSIST Ministries and the ASSIST News Service in Garden Grove, California

ACKNOWLEDEMENTS

Donna, my wife, for loving me enough to see my dream through to the finish.

Abe Clary, for capturing me in thought, (back cover photo) and for making A Narrow Road a reality (front cover photo).

Debbie Schlegel, for taking control of funds, which saw this project to its completion.

Sunshine Root, for the enthusiastic encouragement and smiles

To all the others who believed in me enough to back it, when I couldn't see the end.

Thank you all!

DEDICATED

To my Father in heaven for using me to reach those I can through the gift He gave me.

My wife and friend, Donna, for standing beside me even when I was unsteady

My sons, Joshua and William, my memories keep me going.
(One day I hope to make things right)

My daughter and delight, Anita Rose,
Keep smilin'

My cousin, Janine, Thanks for the continuous push

ASSIST MINISTRIES' Assist News Service & International Press Association, for allowing me to write for them

Debbie Schlegel, for the laughter

TABLE OF CONTENTS

SIGNS ALONG THE ROAD

Chapter One

The narrow road: the path to the heart, entrance to the soul. Can a person make a difference? What if this person is never met or seen? Imaginative? High hopes? The dream stops there. Reality check. Get back to life.

Stop at the place where you are now. Look left. Look right. What's there? Nothing? Keep looking, further on. Close your eyes and you'll see. There it is, beyond the ridge, down the path and around the bend. See it yet?

If you listen for it, you may hear it. Then again, you may not. It depends on what you're hearing with, your ears or your heart? Are you in tune with your surroundings, your inner self? The way is clear. No noises or crowds to distract you. Your name is being called. Your future is there. Destiny is waiting. Take a chance.

Everyone has a narrow road: some are lined with trees some have stones. There are street signs along my road.

Each sign indicates a time when I met up with the voice calling my name, times when I was within touching distance and feeling the presence of the power. Every time I see the signs, I also remember the story of when Christ came near.

At the start, I asked if a person could make a difference, even if unseen. Yes, He can make all the difference, for He is Christ the Lord.

Please, do some searching and try to find your narrow road. You may find the path to the heart, the entrance to the soul. Or better yet, come eye to eye with Christ.

Having been born with Cerebral Palsy, the odds were against me. I didn't walk till I was five. I kept up with my siblings by propelling myself while lying on my belly on a skateboard. Doctors once told me that I'd never walk and if I did walk, my legs wouldn't hold out forever. Over the years, I've had seventeen surgeries. I'm walking like a penguin, but at least I'm walking. Having lost my mother, father and stepfather to different kinds of cancers, by the time I was eighteen, I thought that I was heading nowhere. I wanted the best for myself and knew I'd have to fight much harder to get it. I was born with Cerebral Palsy, but it wasn't going to keep me captive.

As a child, strangers would come up to me and lay hands

on me. They would pray for the healing of my legs yet, when the healings didn't occur, I became bummed. Was I destined to have a hard life? I knew there was a God but I didn't know Him. In 1987, I accepted Christ but still didn't know Him the way I should. I went about doing my own thing. I was in control. I got married in 1990, fathered two sons before it ended in divorce. In 1993, I moved to Washington State to start over.

Never did I think I wouldn't see my children again. That's when I was told by my soon-to-be ex-wife, "I married you because I felt sorry for you."

In early 1994, the divorce became final. In August 1994, I tried to take my life. While in the hospital for attempted suicide with a box-knife to the right wrist, I heard the Lord ask me, "Why did you do this? I didn't ask you to do this."

I met a young lady while attending the Church of the Nazarene. In May of 1995, we were married. Just four months after we met. In November 1996, our daughter was born. The last time I spoke with my ex-wife or either of my sons was in June 1997. That same year, my first book of poetry was published to great acclaim. It sold out within a month. I had finally made it as a writer. But, I still fought with the handicap.

A man once asked me if I was mad at God for punishing me with Cerebral Palsy (CP). I replied, "I'm not mad at God for having done this to me. He wasn't punishing me. There is a

3

ministry going on in my life, even I don't understand. But when the Good Lord is ready, He'll heal my walk. But until then, I will fight the fight and not give in." I felt sincere in saying that but in my heart, I wished that the healing would come soon. I was tired of the struggles that came with this C.P. The next day, I over heard a six-year-old boy ask his mother why I walked the way I do. She told him to ask me. Normally I would have frightened the kid by telling him that I began walking this way after teasing someone who had a handicap. But, I decided to be straight up with this curious kid and face the fact that I had C.P. and couldn't run from the truth. "I was born two months early and didn't get enough oxygen to the brain so now I walk differently from most people." I told him.

"That's okay David, we'll all walk the same in heaven." That simple statement made me cry. I haven't seen that kid since then.

I have written another book of poetry along with my wife, Donna. SECOND CHANCE: Taking the Next Step in Love, was printed in 1999. Books three and four are awaiting printing as I am working on book five of poetry.

When times are tough and things look bleak, we are being tested. Things happen for a reason and we meet the people we do for a reason.

When the cold, uncaring arms of a situation embrace

your whole being, pulling you into the vast blackness of the world, listen to the gentle voice that speaks to your heart. Thus, igniting the ambers of your soul, bringing warmth and meaning to your life.

FROM THE FRYING PAN INTO THE FIRE

1979

Chapter Two

Julie had unknowingly poured lighter fluid on herself while filling a lighter and when she went to light a cigarette, POOF! By the time she got to the shower, she had abstained second and third degree burns to ninety percent of her body. Not long after that, Mom received a letter from our grandmother in Texas stating that grandmother was dying and she wanted us to come out and be with her. So, mom and her boyfriend Jimbo, put Red, Mike, the cat, dog and myself into the Plymouth. All of our belongings were put into a U-Haul and we headed for Texas. I was eleven. I sat in the back seat, looking out the rear window, waving. Life as I knew it was shrinking away...

1985

Chapter Three

In mid October of 1985, my mother had taken ill with colon cancer. The ordeal was a blow. The family was falling apart at the seams, one thread at a time, Mom being the double knot that held us together.

When I found out that our mother was dying, Red and I went to WINNS, where Mike worked to give him the news. Between Red and myself, we decided that I should tell Mike. I guess I could do it easier than Red because I was handling the whole situation better than he was. He wasn't so sure how to explain it to Mike in the right words. We pulled Mike to the rear of the store, between the stock room and the shoes.

I would have preferred to do this in a more private place rather than in this public place. I wasn't in the position to take Mike to the house, so I had to do the best that I could with the place provided.

"Remember. Be easy. We don't know how he's going to take this." Red reminded me.

"I know. But, there's no real way to tell him without him getting hurt. We're all hurt by the news. I will be as subtle as possible. Let's just hope that Mike doesn't black out and lose it right in the shoe department. You just stand there and be a support post for us both." I assured him.

"Why do things always happen when you're not ready for it?" Red asked.

Mike was paged over the intercom to go to the Service Counter. Within a few minutes we saw him walking up between the ladies' shoes and the men's shoes. His face was calm and normal. He had no idea why we were here, nor did he know what we had to tell him. I took a deep breath as Mike neared us. *Here goes nothing,* I thought.

"Hey, Mike. How's your day?" I started

"Fine." He stood firm, his arms folded, legs spread apart for balance and his broad shoulders back. He resembled the statue of David (only with clothes on). He wore blue Five-O-Ones that shaped out the build and the contour of his body. The light pink and white striped shirt was kind of small on him. Mike liked to have his clothes be somewhat small. It showed off his muscles and boldness. I AM THE PILLER OF STRENGTH was written across his forehead. Beyond that, I could see the words CONCEITED AND PRIDEFUL. "What brings you two around here?" He urged.

"Well, Mike, pull up a wall and brace yourself. You're not going to like what I have to say." He leaned on the wall of the stock room and the gloom of discomfort entered his brown eyes. "I will try to tell you this as carefully as possible and I hope that you will handle it." I continued. "This isn't at all easy for me to tell you…" I paused for a breath. "As you know, Mom has become ill and tried to hide the pain and suffering from us. The doctors have told us that she only has about three months to live." I stopped short at the look on his face. Fear was there. He was definitely frightened. I never thought I'd ever fear see take control of "Fearless Manly Mike." I would forever remember his face: a lost child on a strange road leading nowhere on a stormy night.

"We need to stay together and be strong for Mom. She needs all of us to be around her now. It won't be easy, but we have to do it, for her. Now Mike…"

He took off. Red and I had no idea where he was going or what he was doing. We just stood there, lost in the dust of Mike's fear.

"He lost it." Red concluded.

"Yes. I do believe that."

9

"Why do you think he split like that?"

"I would guess that it's his way of dealing with the pain. He was Ross' IDEAL son. Ross put him on a pedestal. After being placed above the rest of us, Ross takes off and we never see him again. That was a blow to Mike. He in turn got close to mom and he fears the fact that she will be going soon. We all have to deal with this in our own ways. Let's just hope that Mike doesn't do anything drastic." We stood there dumbfounded and in wonderment.

*   *   *   *

1986

In the early hours of August first, of eighty-six, at five-thirty in the morning, she passed on. I wasn't aware of her passing until later that day.

Around ten o'clock, I was at work at a small convenience store, next to the Sonic Drive-In, called the Mustang Ice House. I started work about four in the morning. I was sitting behind the counter watching the wedding of Prince Andrew and Sarah "Fergie" Ferguson on the small television. There was a group of customers standing at the fountain machine drawing out a cup of root beer.

There were a few young gentlemen playing pool at the

center pool table and a couple of scraggly kids at the video games.

All was normal for an August day. Suddenly the lady at the fountain began screaming and the two boys that were with her, began laughing hysterically. What the deal was, I didn't know. That was until the lady came up to the counter holding the cup out at arms length. She was frantic.

"What's going on?" I asked.

The woman sat the cup down on the counter and backed away. I turned the volume down on the boob tube and got up from my spot on the stool, leaned forward and took a glance inside the cup. The root beer seemed fine to me. It was foaming as normal. I looked a little closer and saw a very strange movement. The foam was moving!

"ANTS! Oh, my word." I exclaimed.

"Yes, Ants! There are ants coming out with the root beer." The lady finally elaborated.

"I'm sorry, Ma'am. I don't know what to say. This has never happened before. If you would like to get a different soda, I would be happy to give it to you free of charge. I will speak to the management about getting the fountain fixed. Thank you for bringing it to my attention."

"No. Thank you very much all the same. I think I will do without a soda today. Thank you anyhow." She and the two boys turned to exit the store. As I watched them leave, I noticed Red's Chevette pull in the parking lot. His wife, Jacque was with him.

They pulled up to the door. The sadness that they were feeling was unseen by me. I had no sadness whatsoever. I prayed that the terrible pain and suffering my mother was going through would come to a peaceful end. Her passing was supposed to be a joyous time for her and I was asked not to be sad and cry because in the end, she would be in a happier place.

It never entered my mind, at least to me that the end was near. I subconsciously thought that she would go through a miraculous healing and be fine. She wouldn't die and leave me alone. Red and Jacque walked slowly into the store and waited for the customer before them to leave. A few minutes later the store was vacant, except for the people at the pool table.

"What's up?" I asked cheerfully.

Red cast his face downward. "It's over. Mom died this morning at five-thirty."

"No she didn't. You're pulling my leg. She can't be. I would have known."

"She's gone David." Jacque repeated.

I was quiet. It had happened. The end was there. With those sad words they departed.

"We'll be back." Red warned.

Silence filled the room. Even the sound of the pool balls clashing together was silent.

Moments later, the Chevette pulled in again. This time I saw that in Jacque's hands, she held a small ten-inch color television. *My color T.V.! It's true. Mom is dead! Oh, how devastating!* I thought.

When mom went into the nursing home down the street, I had given her my television so that she would have something to do. Not that there was a whole lot she could do. She was always away from herself. One minute she would see that I was standing beside her, holding her hand. The next, she'd pull away from me and ask who I was and what I was doing in her room.

I told myself that when I got the T.V. back, that would mean that she was gone. Here it was. Jacque held the evidence on her lap and the sadness was now evident on their faces. When Red entered the store, I picked up the phone receiver, dialed the home number to the manager and spoke to him of the situation. He said that he would be in soon. Red and Jacque left again. I stood there in total silence. I was fearful of life alone.

When Ted, the manager showed up, he gave me his condolences and I walked blankly next door to give my other boss, Todd, the news. I walked through the door and Todd was standing near the phone, the receiver in his hand. He held it out. "It's for you, David. Someone from California."

"Thank you." I said as I took the receiver from him.

"Hello?"

"This is Johnny."

"Hey Johnny, what's up?"

"Mom's passed on."

"Yeah, I know. How'd you find out before me? I'm only two blocks from where she was."

"She put me down as her closest next of kin. The doctor called me and told me. How are you doing?"

"I'll be fine. She's not hurting anymore. Thank God."

"We'll be there in a few days."

"See ya." I hung up the receiver.

I walked home lost and alone. *I will always remember you the way I last saw you mom. Sorry I wasn't there by your side, but I couldn't bear to have you go in my arms.* I thought as I walked down these once familiar streets. They all seemed strange.

As a child, mom always encouraged us to go to church whenever we could or wanted to, but whether we did or not, that was left up to us. "You don't have to go to church to believe in God." She would tell me. With that statement in mind, I attended church whenever possible. It was fun to learn about our Creator.

I've always believed that there was a God and prayed,

14

but never saw any results. That was, until now. Losing a person to death isn't meant to be a punishment to those who go on living. It's more like a reward for the passing. They did what they were put on this earth to do and when the time comes, that person moves on to another time and another place.

IN AND OUT OF OUR LIVES

Chapter Four

I hadn't seen him in nearly four years. He was some place in Arizona. I knew that much. I had an old address. What were the chances of me finding him there? He moved around like a butterfly. One day he's in Arizona and he could be in Minnesota the next. He wasn't one for staying in one place.

Last October, when my mother was diagnosed with colon cancer, I took a stab in the dark and wrote to the address I had. On a late November afternoon, while I was working at Sonic Drive-In, (the fast food place in town), this brown van pulls up in the vacant lot next door.

I was so mad at him because there were many things that he did to my whole family that I could never forgive him for. To see that I had gotten through to him with my letter, I was glad. He was here now, and that was what mattered. I didn't want to

16

go through this alone.

Red and his wife, Jacque was here, but they were trying to deal with this in ways that were so different, that we couldn't console each other. My father would console me. He would help me through this.

That's what father's were for. He may not pop in but once every couple of years but he was here for me now.

I went out to welcome him with open arms. "Hi, Dad. Thanks for coming. I wasn't sure you got my letter. I really need some help." I leaned up against the driver side window.

He smiled. "Hi, David. This is Velda." He introduced me to the lady in the van. I shook her hand. "I got your letter and headed out right away."

"That's good." I said.

"I didn't come to stay. I came to take you from here, now." He had a stern look on his face. I glanced over at Velda. She said nothing.

In utter and complete shock, I backed away from the van. I nailed my father to his seat with my eyes. (At that moment, even though I was just barely two months being seventeen, I felt like I had grown up at least four more years.) I remember saying, "What? I asked you here so that I would have someone to lean on when my mother, YOUR WIFE, died and you have the nerve to tell me that? Well, Ross, forget it!" I was roaring

17

mad. "Go back to Arizona. I don't need you!"

His eyes widened at my calling him by his name. I no longer saw him as a dad or a father. From that day on, he was a stranger: a stranger with no place in my heart. Now, I know why I hated him so. He was a cold-hearted man.

LAID TO REST

Chapter Five

An older gentleman walked in and inquired as to whom my brother Red and I were. He then pulled us aside and asked us to sign a piece of paper. I later realized that what we signed was a legal consent document. That which in itself stated that we released our mother's remains to be cremated. When that realization hit me, I felt as though I had signed her death warrant. What an awful feeling to have to live with.

Everyone left after they gave their condolences. The family members regrouped outside. Mom wasn't outside like I had hoped. She really was dead. What a downer. I noticed that Johnny was carrying a small box to his car. I went over to Tama and asked, "Who would give a gift to Johnny in a brown box?"

"That's not a gift." Tama said softly.

"Then what is it?"

"That's mom's ashes. Inside that brown box is a brown plastic box. Johnny's going to take the ashes back to California and spread them on Tapo Hill." She confirmed with tears in her eyes.

"Oh," was all I could say. I looked off to the street sign that read: BURNETT, TEXAS FUNERAL HOME. THE PLACE TO PUT YOUR SORROWS TO REST.

THE SHOCK OF REALITY
Chapter Six

Our mother had passed and all the family came to Texas to the funeral, everyone but Clifford and Julie. We hadn't seen one another in eight years. That was a long time to be apart.

The only conclusion they could agree on was that Julie was off in her own world looking for a fix. She had no idea that mom was ill. That was real sad. Anyway, after I had been in California for a couple of weeks, Tama, Eddie and I went to visit Julie. I was excited.

"You know where she's at?" I asked with anticipation.

"She lives in Bakersfield. She rents a house on Skeat Street. It's about a two hour drive from here."

"Sounds cool."

"Wait 'til you see Wendy. She's ten now. She acts older though because she has to take care of Julie. It's not the kind of life for a young girl." She ended sadly.

"The last time I saw her, she was three."

"This will be a surprise for her too. She has no idea you're here or that mom died. I'm hoping that when she sees you, it will dawn on her." Tama stared me in the face.

"Isn't that a little harsh?" I asked, searching for that soft glow in her eyes.

"Maybe. We tried to tell her, but we couldn't find her."

Nothing more was said the whole way there until we turned down the awful looking street. I had never seen such a place. I read about them, but never knew they existed. The yards and the street were covered with trash. The small children ran about half naked. Their hair unwashed and their bodies had what looked like three layers of dirt on them. It was putrid and sad to see this. *How could anyone choose to live like this?* I couldn't remember my childhood being this bad. *Surely, Julie didn't live here!* I thought to myself. The last I heard she was married to a biker that she had intended mom to hook up with. His name was Paul and they lived in a nice neighborhood. Julie was going to beauty school then. She was a very good beautician. She had followed in my father's steps and was making something of her life.

"Is Julie still married to Paul? What happened to the nice house they had?" Curiosity was getting the better of me.

"Yes, they're still married, but they've been separated for the past five years. Paul moved out of state with Becky and Harley, and Julie and Wendy live here." We pulled up along side the curb and got out.

"Where do they live?"

"There." Eddie pointed to a grungy old yellow and brown house that the paint was pealing off of.

I cocked an eyebrow. "You've got to be joking!" I stood there, mouth open. This young girl with dark brown hair and olive colored skin came running out the door. She threw her small boned arms out hugging Tama.

"Mom! Aunt Tama's here." She yelled back at the house. No one appeared in the doorway. This girl was in her early teens, or so I thought.

"David." Tama said with a smile. "This is your niece, Wendy."

I was astonished. All I could say as I looked into her green eyes was, "Boy, have you grown. The last time I remember seeing you, you were only this tall." I put my hand down by my knees. "You look great." I added after we embraced in a tight hug. The three of us walked up to the house. Eddie followed behind us. It was nice to have family again.

The house was in shambles. There was an older looking man on the couch. I didn't catch his name. There were piles of clothes all over the place. Food lay on the tables, both in the living room and in the kitchen. Dishes stacked about. There were books on shelves, lots of them. Did Julie read a lot?

There were familiar works. Mainly V.C. Andrews' novels: Flowers in the Attic, Petals in the Wind, If There be Thorns in Heaven. I had read all of these books and had become a great fan of the author. I was very fond of S.E. Hinton and Stephen King. I inwardly hoped and prayed that some day, I would write great novels of fiction myself. That was my dream, to be a well-known writer and give back to the world of books what it had given to me.

The bedroom door, which was to the right of the living room, was closed. Wendy knocked. "Mom, Aunt Tama and Da..." Tama motioned for her not to say anything about me yet. "...and Eddie are here." She then went about picking up the clothes and dishes of food and putting them all in their rightful places.

The door started to open and Tama pushed me aside and stepped into the room, closing the door again. Minutes later Tama resurfaced and went and stood next to Eddie who was sitting in the recliner.

I stood there waiting...and waiting. It seemed like forever. Finally Julie put her hands to her head and screamed, "Oh my God. I don't believe it. David, you're here." She began to cry tears of joy as she hugged me. "Look at you. You're not that little boy who use to lay on a skateboard and push himself around trying to keep up with the rest of us anymore."

"No. I'm all grown up." I said as I fought back the tears, even through the terrible secret I held inside. I returned her warm embrace.

"Man, what a trip. Tama, look at him." She instructed with tears streaming down her cheeks. "Wow, man. Look Dweebo," she went over and slapped the man lying on the couch. "Look. This is my little bother." Julie glanced over at me, "Well, he ain't so little any more. I'm happy you're here." Julie took me by the hand. "Looky here, David." She pulled me into the room. I turned to look at Tama. There were tears in her eyes now. I closed the door.

Again, she proclaimed that she was happy to see me. "I can't imagine what would bring you back here from Texas." She stated.

If you only knew, I thought

I kept a smile on my face as best I could as she pointed out all the small ceramic knick-knacks that mom had given to her before we left. "You kept all those little puppies, angels, flowers and things that mom gave you?" I asked with surprise.

"Yeah, I even wrote you guys several letters. See?" Julie pulled out a file folder filled with letters that were addressed to mom and I. "I never mailed them though. I wish I had."

Yeah, I wish you had also. I said sadly to myself as I glanced around the room. I saw this painting on the wall above Julie's bed. It was one that our mom had painted the year Wendy was born. It was of a clown. He had a large red smile, a red nose, green hair and sad blue eyes on an orangish-peach back ground. Wendy was mom's first grandbaby. In the bottom right corner of the painting was a baby's footprint. There were lots of memories within the painting. It would mean even more to Julie when she realizes why I was here.

"I'm sorry I never mailed the letters, but I was too busy buying dope and crack and whatever else I could get my needful hands on."

"I'm sorry that you didn't have a better life. I love you and God loves you." I reassured her with a hug. We went back into the living room.

"So, guys. Where's mom? Did she come with you or did she stay in Texas?"

Tama and I looked at each other.

"Julie, can you show me around outside?" I took her hand and walked out to the curb. "I have something to tell you and it's not gonna be easy." We started down the street. "I love you Julie, you know that right?"

"Yeah." She stopped me at the corner. "What?"

Needing more time to think I said, "Is there a store within walking distance that sells Abba Zabba candy bars?"

"You still eat those? When you were little you'd bug me endlessly to buy them for you when I went to the store." She paused. "There's a store at the other corner. We can go there."

"Yes, I still eat those. They're great." We laughed. I didn't say anything else until on the way back from the store.

"Do you realize why I'm here?" I tried to be gentle.

"You're here visiting. That reminds me. Where's mom? Why didn't she come? I'm sure she would have loved to see Wendy."

"I know for a fact she would have loved that, but Julie..." we stopped at the truck in the front of the house. I held her at arms length and against the truck. "Julie, I'm sorry, but Mom died last month." I pulled her towards me and held tightly.

She cried, "Oh, my God! No. Not mom!"

I pressed her head to my shoulder. "It's alright. She went easy. She's with the Lord now. She's in no more pain."

Julie straightened up and looked me in the eyes. "Why didn't anyone tell me? I would have gone. I wanted to see her." her eyes now swollen with tears.

"Tama told me that they looked all over for you, but they had no luck in finding you. They left messages and everything."

"They knew where I was. I was here. All my friends know how to find me…" She bowed her head, "…I can't believe Mom's dead." Raising her head she asked, "How?"

"In October of eighty-five she was diagnosed with colon cancer. She went through treatment of chemo and the doctors said she only had three months. She lasted until August of this year."

"Who all went to Texas?"

"Everyone except you and Clifford."

"Why didn't he go?"

"He's wanted by the police and didn't want to chance going to jail."

We hugged once more then walked into the house. "My God, Tama, is it true?" Julie asked as she went to embrace her.

"Yes. I'm sorry you had to find out like this, but I thought that if you saw David, you would know that something was wrong. After all, he's been with mom for the last eight years."

"No. It didn't dawn on me."

"She went fine. She went a happy grandma." Tama grinned.

"What?" Julie asked confused. She glanced over at Eddie and me.

"I have no idea what she's talking about Julie, so don't

28

look at me." I said.

"When I went out there to see mom, the first time, before she died...well, I found out that I was pregnant." She was glowing.

"Really?" Julie exclaimed with excitement.

"Praise God!" I yelled with laughter and glory.

"What?" They both said in unison.

"Mom passed away. She's with the Lord. And now, there's a baby on the way to bless the family." Julie, Tama and Wendy looked at me as though I was speaking a foreign language.

"What's that mean?" Wendy asked.

"For each person that passes on, there's a child born."

*　　*　　*　　*

I was just about at the apartment when Amanda came running around the corner. "Uncle David!" she yelled. "I missed you today!" She jumped into my arms almost knocking me over.

"Oh, boy! There's my sister's little girl."

The miracle of life.

HIDDEN STRENGTH

Chapter Seven

I had given the kids their breakfast that morning and it was around two in the afternoon when they were finishing up with their lunch as Julie finally rolled out of bed. She dragged her skinny five foot-two inch framed body down the stairs.

Dressed in her boyfriend's white T-shirt and a pair of his boxers (with the front hole sewed closed), she casually stepped into the kitchen and reached for the refrigerator door. In doing this, she revealed the light purple track marks.

"Where's all the Dr. Pepper?" Julie asked as she sleepily looked over the contents of the icebox.

"The kids had it for lunch." I said firmly. My sister's uncaring still fresh in my mind. *How could she do that to herself?* I thought. *It's gross.* The door shut.

I rolled my eyes in frustration and took a deep breath.

"Well, if you didn't sleep in until two and chose to get up with the rest of us, you would have gotten some." I stood my ground. That was something I very seldom did. I had no guts. Where this courage suddenly came from, I didn't know. All I knew was I had to act on what was there. There wasn't anyone there to fight this battle. I stood alone. God had given me the strength and now I had to face the giant.

When we had our battles, we would handle it one of two ways: we would walk out of the room when the other one came in or we gave the silent treatment for any given length of time. Our fights were hardly ever physical but mostly always verbal. Most of the time, words hurt more than anything. Some situations arose though, where the anger took over and the battle was on.

Julie knew full well what I was referring to. Julie's daughter, Wendy and Tama's little Amanda cleared their lunch plates and vanished like smoke. They knew what was going on. These confrontations were becoming very regular. The discussions were the same, but the intensity was continually changing.

"I had a long night. Get off my back. I do what I want." She reminded me calmly.

As the saying goes: 'It's always calm before the storm.'

"That's just it. You do whatever you want and no one

else matters." I walked into the living room. The kids left the front door and the windows open. I should have closed them, but I didn't. Maybe if the neighbors heard the fight, it would jar Julie into reality. Maybe make her face her responsibilities as a mother. Then again, knowing my sister the way I do, it probably wouldn't phase her one bit, would it?

Maybe I just didn't understand what she was going through. If only she'd help us to understand her situation. See it through her eyes, in her point of view. Tell us how she feels. If she prayed, that would help her more than she knows. She has a good heart. It's the rest of her that's messed up. It's those drugs.

Lord God, I pray that you will release my sister from the arms of doing wrong. I stood in silence, hearing the words as they ran threw my head. I ended the prayer with a quiet amen.

For a brief second, I glanced at the stairs. I thought to run, but my feet would not move. I looked at Julie and thought, *there must be a reason I cannot run. There is something that has to be said and I'm here to tell it.* I tried to push the thought out of the way so that I could face her clearly. The harder I pushed, the more I thought them. I then realized that I wasn't really alone. God had to be working through me. I wouldn't have faced Julie otherwise.

I felt my anger surfacing as I continued to face her. I

knew that the truth was going to come out. I was going to open my mouth and the words were about to flow. I just hoped that I wouldn't stick my foot in it.

"You're out all night with your 'friendly connections' doing only God knows what and probably enjoying every painful minute of it. Then you sleep all day!" I was beginning to lose my composure. My once muffled anger was now at a head. My legs were trembling. I wasn't weakening, I was mad. I tried to look at her but she wouldn't look back.

"That's my business. Keep your nose out of it!" She demanded as she filled her glass with water.

"It would be easier to stay out of it if you wouldn't bring it into our home." I leaned on the couch for a steady support. Little did Julie know, but God was there for spiritual support.

"I don't bring it into the apartment." She denied. But the look in her eyes said different. Suddenly, I remembered the last time I saw her 'load up'.

"Bull, Julie. I got up this morning to feed the kids and as I left my room I glanced over to your door…"

"So." she interrupted with a low voice. "My door was closed."

"I only wished it was!" I disagreed. "Seeing you at the desk with your right arm laid out across it…and the rubber band tie you used made me sick…" I froze in time at the thought of this morning.

"Why didn't you go on and ignore it? It wasn't something you should have seen?" She walked over to the counter and refrained from coming closer. Why she did so, I could not have imagined at the time. Temperatures were rising fast. A volcano was about to erupt. Unbeknown to her, I was very glad she stayed there. Who would I be kidding? Julie may be skinny, but she still had more body balance and strength than I did. I had the strength and faith of God, that, I was aware of. Emotionally and spiritually, for now, I had her beat. Physically, I was no match for her. We balanced one another out: I had something she didn't. I had Jesus. I prayed that she'd receive Him. He was already there for her, she just had to accept Him and believe.

I continued to clean the slate.

"I'm glad it was me and not one of the kids. Not that it matters. Not to you anyway," I paused, waiting for a reply. None came. I continued. "They know that you inject yourself into a world where only you and Satan can live. You're afraid to live in reality. And, that's sad because when the drugs don't take over, you are a very beautiful person. Give that life to the devil and take the hand of God. Close the door on temptation to do wrong and do right. Take back control of your life. Ask God for help. He'll help you. We want to help you, but we can't."

"We want to help you through this. The first step has to be yours. You're going to want to have to quit. Do it for yourself." The room fell silent. It was a scary silence.

"We all see the difference." I went on. "Even little Amanda notices that you're not the same Aunt JuJu she loves. Face it Julie, you are only fooling yourself. You're certainly not fooling us. And, you're really out on a limb if you think you are pulling one over on God." I waited quietly.

Julie gazed at me puzzled and confused. "NO!" she blurted out. "Amanda doesn't know." The look of shock and surprise overcame her.

"Yes, Julie, she does know. Granted she doesn't realize exactly what it is you do, but she does sense that there is something wrong in the way you behave from one moment to the next. Why do you think she split out of here with Wendy? In case you didn't notice, Julie, they took off out of here like skyrockets on the Fourth of July. Amanda may only be three, but give her some credit. She's not dumb." Tears began to fall from my eyes as I belted out the truth. It was cold and hard for me to say, but much more difficult for her to hear.

The darkness in her life was being thrust off balance by the light of truth. There was no more living in Satan's lair. In order to win the battle, she'd have to come out fighting.

It wouldn't be easy, yet it could be done. The step was

hers. I felt sorry for her.

In the back of my mind, I subconsciously wished I hadn't been the one who saw that needle this morning. I also wished that I hadn't been chosen to face Julie at this moment. If it could have been anyone else, Amanda's mother, our older sister, Tama would be doing it. *Where was Tama when I needed her? At work? I should be at work.* I thought.

There was a reason why I stayed home. I couldn't quite put my finger on it. I knew that God had his hand on this day. It was planned for me. I understood that I shouldn't question His motives for having things happen certain ways, but I couldn't help but to wonder.

Why me Lord? Why not someone stronger?

With those questions in mind, I stood against the couch and proceeded to say the only unheard of saying that we all feared. Even Julie. "Heck, Julie, for all you know, you might have caught AIDS! Have you ever thought of that?" Shock overtook me. I was taken by surprise. I would have done without that last phrase. It was too late. The cold truth had been spoken. We felt the icy Arctic winds blow through us like a knife through butter. The apartment grew cold as we were submerged into the chilling waters of the truth.

As we returned to surface of the waters of words, I realized that as I opened my mouth, a brother-sister trust was

36

broken.

Julie raised the glass of water she held eyeing me like a hungry hawk about to tackle his prey as she hurled it towards me. Like a comet, it came at me. I ducked out of its path and sought refuge in the cushions of the couch. She yelled, "You bastard!" She glanced at the door thinking of what to say that was nice, yet blunt. Having come to the conclusion that all she didn't want was the neighbors to hear was heard. There was no hiding. She was open for the outside world to see. "How dare you accuse me of having AIDS? You don't know. Who are you to judge? Who are you to judge me or my life?" Tears fell from her eyes. I just opened the glass casing she had built around her life. To her, the only ones who were allowed in were her connections and the devil. She was wrong. God was there…waiting.

The glass shattered against the wall above my head, as the love Julie and I held so strong, shattered before me. In that instant I was sorry. Sorry for her, and also for myself for what I had said. Nothing I could ever do would repair the damage I caused. I too, began to pray for the strength and goodness to come out of this mess.

There is always a silver lining behind each storm cloud. Where was the light?

I stood dumbfounded as I blankly saw Julie run up the

stairs. *All I did was speak the truth,* I thought. I sat silently for a moment before realizing that I was wet. I found it ironic to be covered in water and at the same time, be submerged in regret. *Lord, help her.* I thought. I sat gazing out the window.

What will the neighbors think?

Later, after Tama came home, the batter was on, again. This time I sat at the sidelines with the kids. There was one thing I wasn't aware of. Apparently, while Julie was in the rest room, (recuperating from my devastating blow) her daughter, Wendy went through her mother's closet.

Not really wanting to find what she knew was there, but felt she had to make us aware of, an intravenous syringe. Empty, of course, but nonetheless there. Wendy took it to Tama, knowing that was the right thing to do. Sooner or later though, she will pay for her nosiness.

I sat there hoping that Tama wouldn't get upset. She had a right to, if she did, it was her apartment. Julie, Wendy and I were there because we couldn't afford to be on our own. So, we moved in with Tama. She could have kicked us out at any given time. That wasn't her way. She, being the kind-hearted person she is, would rather face the problem and straighten it out.

She was the strong one of the bunch.

Above all that though, she was a month-and-a-half pregnant. There was an unborn child to consider. Would she stay cool? Not Tama. She could handle anything, especially these situations with Julie. Everything was going to be fine. I had faith in that. I prayed for help. It couldn't hurt.

Like a flash, Tama was up the stairs and at the bathroom door within seconds. Moments later, their yelling and screaming were amplified. They were coming down stairs. Amanda huddled on the couch, Wendy stood by the dining room table and I stood by the phone. My two sisters were like pit bulls. Instead of having locked jaws, they had handfuls of hair, as they rolled down the two short flights of stairs. BOOM... BOOM... BOOM!!!

They stood face to face at the bottom of the stairs. Like day and night they continued their fight, verbally. "I've told you over and over that I didn't want drugs brought into my house! Don't you understand that there are children living here? I don't want them seeing it or getting into it." Tama was holding nothing back. Again, the truth was being told. I would think that if two people told me the same story, I'd think twice about what I was doing. That's me...Not Julie.

"I know, you've said that! But it's my life!" was all Julie could say. She glanced over at twelve-year old Wendy.

"She's another reason I won't allow drugs in this house." Tama continued with firmness and tears in her hazel eyes.

"Wendy has been put through enough for her lifetime.

She's been putting up with this crud for a long time. Do you want to her end up like you? Do you want to lose her? Because, let me warn you, if you keep this up, the authorities will remove her from your care. Do you want Wendy to grow up around this? I don't want any of that. I don't need any part of it. If you can't see that, well then, I guess you're lost to your addiction." She placed her hand over her belly.

I said a small prayer for peace between us and hoped for the child Tama carried. Then out of the blue I started to think of what the neighbors were thinking: *Where's the popcorn? It's round two over at Julie's house.* I wanted to laugh at the thought, but decided against it.

Julie looked Tama in the face, "No, that isn't what I want for Wendy or Amanda. That is the reason I sent my two little ones, Becky and Harley to be with their father. I understand that I've put Wendy through heck and I'm sorry. I'm sorry that I do it around here. I'm sorry that I do it at all. But I can't stop. It hurts too much." She placed her hands to her face and wept like a child.

"Then I'll help you. We'll all help you, Julie, but you have to want the help." Tama offered, then waited. Julie gave a few little sniffles, but no response. Tama moved her thin frame past Julie and went to the table. Wendy backed up against the closed front door. Tama armed herself with the empty syringe, took a deep breath and faced Julie once more.

"Where is the rest of it Julie?" she questioned. "Give it up. Give it all up to me so that I can get rid of it. If you want our help, this is how it has to be." Tama held up the syringe.

Give it up to Jesus. I thought.

"Where is it?" Tama repeated a little louder.

"It's all gone. I have no more." Julie confessed.

The two gladiators had squared off. Light was prevailing over dark. It was as though a light switch was turned on. POOF! No more darkness. Then with a 360-degree turn, Julie faced her daughter. For the moment, the rest of us vanished as Wendy waited for the punishment she knew was coming. She showed no fear facing the woman she loved. She wasn't going to lose her mother.

Why couldn't Julie see that?

"How dare you go through my stuff?" Julie yelled. Wendy waited without flinching for the punch line.

SMACK!! Wendy hit the door as her mother's hand crossed her face then fell into a slump in the corner.

Reaching her hands up to protect her face as she was slapped again. Julie began to kick and cuss. Tama tried to stop the abuse, but Wendy raised her hand knowing her mother would run out of steam.

I couldn't watch this outrage go on. It was unbelievable

how Wendy took the wrath of her mother-gone-mad. I picked up the receiver, "Julie stop this now or I'm calling the cops."

The hitting stopped, but Julie's arrow-like stare targeted on me. I began to dial...

"Yes. Can you..." Julie came at me with enough force to knock the wind out of me. My grip still on the receiver, but my words was cut short. My sister pulled the receiver free and repeatedly beat me on the head. Raising my arms for protection, I began to yell at her in anger, not pain. I understood then how Wendy did it. When you're that mad, you'll hold up to anyone.

Tama had her turn. Wendy had hers and although Julie and I went at it earlier, it was my turn again.

When Julie realized that the phone wasn't hurting me, she grabbed me by the hair and thrust my head into the wall. OUCH!! Now that hurt. I felt a headache coming on.

"Ouch. Son of a biscuit!" I yelled in pain.

Julie's grip loosened. Before Tama could do or say anything, Julie ran past Amanda and up the stairs.

Amanda's big brown eyes followed her JuJu up the stairs. The little one was crying. In all the confusion, everyone forgot about Amanda on the couch watching it all. Amanda ran over to her mom saying tearfully, "I hate JuJu, Mommy." She grabbed her mommy around the neck and squeezed as tightly as her little arms could allow. "Did she hurt you?" she asked.

42

"No, Amanda. Mommy's not hurt. Thank you for asking, Sweetie, I love you too." Tama returned the hug and then placed her bony hand over her belly, rubbing gingerly. Seeing this, little Amanda bent over so that she was face to face with Tama's stomach. She lifted Tama's shirt enough to expose her navel and said, "Are you okay in there, baby Brother? Did Aunt JuJu hurt you, little brother?" We all started laughing at the sincere concern Amanda showed.

She must really want a little brother." I stated.

"Well…" Tama started to explain.

"Well, Uncle David, I really would like a little sister." Amanda interrupted, "but mommy says it will be a boy." She glanced up at her mommy, "Right?" Her smile melted our hearts.

"Right. Now, do me a favor. Go upstairs and give Aunt JuJu a hug and tell her that you love her, okay?" Tama smiled.

"Okay, Mom." Amanda headed toward the stairs.

We sat there listening to the pitter-patter of her little feet as she raced across the second floor hall. "JuJu, I'm coming!" she warned.

I looked deeply into Tama's hazel eyes. I'm sorry for having put you through all this pain and frustration." I reached out and took hold of her hand.

"It's okay, I don't mind. The pain is well worth the

frustration if it will help her see what she's doing. We can help her but the first step has to be made by her."

"I pray that God will guide her to choose the right steps before it's too late." I stated with conviction.

Wendy and Tama gleamed at me as though I had lost my mind. We, as a family, have an unspoken understanding that God will help all who ask for His help. I looked at Wendy and for the first time, realized that her face was swollen and red.

"Are you okay, Wendy?" I asked.

She volunteered no response, just sat there, crying the silent tears of a scared child.

Later that evening, I was sitting on one of the swings outside the apartment complex. I dragged my feet in the sand, staring at the stars. The night sky was so clear that it seemed as though I was looking through a glass at the stars that hung like fire flies on invisible strings, so peaceful, so open, so free.

It would be nice to feel that sort of freedom, but there was none for me at this time. What a devastating feeling. It was so uncomfortable. I couldn't wait to get rid of the evilness that engulfed my whole being. I wanted to be set free from the pain, hurt and lies.

I searched the sand beneath me for the answers to the freedom the stars hadn't provided. I found, instead, a jagged piece of glass. Without thinking of the consequences or thinking at all, I picked it up and befriended the sandy thing. I turned my right wrist over, palm side up, and began working the glass over the veins that pumped outward. It seemed like the veins were reaching out to touch the glass themselves. That wasn't the case.

I had hold of my wrist just beneath the hand and started curling my fingers inward, then stretching them outward, until the veins were full of blood. I continued to do this, with the intentions of ending all the pain and frustrations for about five minutes.

Tama walked up.

"How you doing' David?" She asked from the edge of the sand.

"Okay, I guess." I gave a small smile.

"Amanda wants you to come tuck her into bed. Tonight is your night Uncle David." She smiled and went back to the apartment.

I glanced up at the stars again, closed my eyes, them back at my first attempt to end everything: pain and happiness, all together.

That's it. Leave little Amanda and her sweet ways behind. Do exactly what JuJu is doing. Trying to leave reality to hide from the hurt. That's dumb. What am I doing? I thought. I looked again at what I had started. Traces of blood began to appear beneath the skin. The blood wasn't flowing, but the everlasting scars were set. I would never forget what Satan wanted me to do. NO MORE!

Jesus bled for me. He bled for us all, the people of the world. *Jesus Christ, I open my heart to you. Please, forgive me and those that I love for the sins we have committed against You.* I though.

I saw Amanda running towards me. "Come on, Uncle David. I want you to tuck me in." She yelled as she ran up to me and gave me a hug. I looked into her child brown eyes and smiled. "I love you Amanda."

"I love you too, Uncle David." She smiled back.

As she took my hand and led me home, I said aloud, "Thank you God." I wiped the tears away. As we entered the apartment, Tama asked. "How's your wrist?" She smiled slightly. I looked at her with surprise.

God bless hidden strength.

FAITH AWAKENING

Chapter Eight

Since that night, three weeks ago, Julie, her boyfriend and Wendy moved out. They found this old run down shack of a house a few miles from the apartment. That was good. Julie got a job working the graveyard shift at the local Circle K at the corner of their street.

Julie seemed to be happy there. She was finally making an effort to the life she had a second chance to live. She was bursting with joy every time I saw her. That was until one deserted quiet night, while she was bent down behind the counter filing paperwork. A car passed by the front of the store. People were having a joyride through town. A shot rang out and the plate glass front window was pierced. The bullet passed over Julie's head and lodged itself in the beer case at the back of the store. Boy, was she lucky. She could have been killed. Thank

God for that. Julie quit the next day.

The house they moved to was real cozy looking: a fence around the yard, a fireplace in the center of the living room. The kitchen, which was painted lime green, was off to the left side as you walk through the front door. The living room was a faded tan. The single room in the house was off to the right. It was yellow with big windows. Unlike the rest of the home, this room was full of bright light. The bathroom was to the right of the room. It resembled a jail cell, very small and again it was painted a lime green. The combination of colors grossed me out. I became ill at the sight of it. Whoever had this house last, had no sense of color coordination.

"Nice house. Great paint job. I love the choice of colors. Who's your decorator?" I asked with a disgusted smirk. Julie came out of the bedroom and laughed at my forwardness.

"The owners did it. Do you really like them? I hate it myself. I think it's ugly?" She smiled, gave me a hug. "How you doing, David? Here, sit down." She pointed at the kitchen table. She's come a long way since the fight. Calmness settled within her.

"Are you using?" I asked, wondering.

"Yeah, but not so much."

"Well, you're looking better." I complimented.

I could see a great difference between then and now. She

put on more weight. Smiled more, and handled herself in a better manner. I guess she thinks getting a job and taking on the responsibilities made her think of all that she was willing to give up. I knew Jesus had a whole lot to do with the new strength she felt. Julie knew He was the reason. She wouldn't admit it. Hey, everyone has to start somewhere.

"Do you mind me asking where do you get your stuff?"

"The owners."

"Where do they live?"

"Next door. I can't say I like the idea."

"Why's that?" I asked, fearful about finding out.

"They're full fledged junkies. You thought I was bad a month ago. David, these people are that way all the time. I've worked so hard to get this far and the thought of having temptation next door really irks me. The rent is cheap."

"How much?"

"Four hundred. We pay the bills. That part is cool now that I've been working at the liquor store down at the end of town, The Fox Tail. But, my job isn't solely for bill paying. Living here has its price." She looked at me. Her hair was golden brown, not dingy. Her eyes open and alert not dilated. She was beginning to beauty up. Her skin was gaining color and best of all her battle wounds were starting to heal, most of them anyway. It was good.

"I'm so proud of you for coming this far. I don't like the idea of you using, but I understand that you have to take it one step at a time. Thank God." I commended her.

The thing I liked was that we were becoming close again. Not as before, but that was lost for good in the web of our past. The newness we felt for each other had a light on it. We still had our disagreements, but who doesn't? I've always loved her and now that she's made some changes, I've gained a new respect for her. I love Jesus for His guidance and help.

"Where's that boyfriend of yours. Or should I ask?" I gave her a suspicious glance.

"You guess it...He's over with them scoring a deal. We don't use that much any more, thank God, but he deals with it some. I don't fight with him. It keeps them off our backs if we're late on the rent."

"Sis, that's not good." I pointed my finger.

"I didn't say I liked it. I can't complain, but I don't like it. I just stay quiet." She shrugged her shoulders in a way that wasn't satisfying.

"Is this how you feel? Or are you pulling my chain?"

"No, David, I'm not pulling your chain...well, sort of, I suppose."

"What's that mean?"

"I told my dweeb of a boyfriend that he'd better get off

the dope or I'm going to leave him here in this paraphernalia nest. I would like to get totally clean and have a new life." She pointed to a plaque on the wall as she went to the sink. She reached for the water faucet and a glass.

The title of the plaque read 'Footprints in the Sand'; I smiled as I watched every move she made. I asked, "What do you mean when you say '…have a new life…' I can take that all kinds of ways. Tell me what you mean." My hope was rising.

She set the glass down on the counter and laughed. Neither one of us had forgotten that day. "I'm not going to throw it at you. I promise."

I got up and started to leave.

"I have to get going. Ed asked if I could watch Amanda after their day at the park. He has plans tonight while Tama's at work. I didn't ask questions. I just said, 'yes'".

"Come on. Stay. I'll have Wendy go watch her. I want to talk to you. How often do you and I actually talk?"

"Almost never. Unless, of course, you're on one of those binges." I raised my left eyebrow.

Wendy was just entering the house. "Hi mom, hi Uncle David."

"Hi Wendy." I yelled.

"Hi Wendy. Can you do me a favor and go over to Aunt Tama's and watch Amanda so that David and I can talk?"

"Sure, I'm on my way." She took off out the door. Apartment bound.

Julie sat back down and started, "I know you've been waiting for me to say this. I've been meaning to tell you." She closed her eyes and took a deep breath. I couldn't stop smiling. I was feeling good that she was coming clean with her situation and with me of all people. She continued. "I want to stop living this drug depressed life. I've lived it for too long and put everyone that I love through hell. My life, as it stands, stinks. For many years, up to the last few months, I've put my connections and the needles first. David," she paused, "what I'm trying to say is that since that day…three weeks ago, I've been feeling different. I don't know how to explain it. You know? It's just that…there's been this pain. Not a hurting pain or even a withdrawal pain. It's more like a yearning or a growing pain."

For the first time in two years, I finally witnessed the joy that Jesus can bring even though you don't know it's Him. Julie was crying, not her regular pity cry. I had built up a resistance to that. She was weeping waterfalls, hard-core. I felt the happiness she showed. I smiled.

"Praise God. That urging isn't a worldly want." I took a hold of her hand, squeezing it tightly. "He wants you to let this demonic life go. Live for the Lord. Do what He would have you do; which are the right things, the things that will glorify Him.

Ask for His guidance in doing His will. You have to want His help in order for that to happen."

"What do you mean?" her eyes full of wonder.

"When you pray, ask to be used by Him. Don't tell Him to do anything. If He feels you can handle it and it's right, He'll give it to you. He may not answer your prayer in the instant. Believe He is near and hold your faith and He will take care of you. I realize He hears all prayers, no matter how short or long, from anywhere. But, I feel aside from prayer and worship with other fellow believers in a church, I feel much closer to the Lord if I'm alone. If there's someone or something I need to pray for, I always wait until I'm alone with Him and then ask for His help. In Matthew 6:5-6 it says:

'When you pray, don' be like the hypocrites. They love to stand in the synagogues and on the street corners and pray loudly. They want people to see them pray. I tell you the truth. They already have their full reward. When you pray, you should go to your room and close the door. Then pray to your Father who cannot bee seen. Your Father can see what is done in secret, and He will reward you.' (The Everyday Bible. The New Century Version.) I sat quietly, holding her hand, choosing my words.

I wanted Julie to want to see what He had in store for her. After a moment of peace, I continued. "I'm very glad to

53

see that you now want this. We all love you dearly. We don't want to lose you. You may be in pain at times and during those times you can come to us. We're your family and as such, we will stick with you. I want you to know that we're only human. We tend to get real tired of the same old song and dance. 'The Boy Who Cried Wolf' as the saying goes.

"Jesus has placed it upon my heart to tell you to lean on Him as heavy as you did that needle. We are there for you. The Lord is there for you. When the door is open, listen to Him. We will listen to you, but when we've had enough of your backsliding and broken promises, we get up and tell you that you're on your own. Jesus will always be there for you through all things, good and bad, as long as you are willing to have Him as your personal Lord and Savior. Once you've asked Him to guide your life don't deny him. He may close the door.

"I'm not saying that He won't watch over you. He is forever watching over the world. What I am saying is that His grace will cover you as long as you are alive. Turning away will only blind you from seeing His ever-extended hand. You will fall harder than before. You will begin to feel like a rubber ball being bounced to no end. Things will seem to go wrong until you accept the Lord's guidance. Ask Him to use you to do His will, for yourself and the good of others. Ask for His forgiveness and that He wash away your sins with the blood of

His Son, Jesus. From that day forth, if you do what He will have you do, you shall have a place in the Kingdom of God. Don't willingly go out and do something wrong and then ask for forgiveness. He doesn't work that way. Do what is right and He will take care of you."

"Thank you for telling me this. I knew you would understand." She squeezed my hand and released it. "You know, I really admire you for standing up to me that day. That took guts. I could have rung your neck, you had me that mad."

I put my hand to the back of my head, "I know."

"I'm sorry for putting your head into the wall. Are you okay?"

"I'll be fine. I get headaches when I see the hole that's in the wall. I survived; I knew I was going to get something out of you. I was scared to death to face you. I hadn't realized it until that moment when we were facing off, that God wanted me to be truthful with you. I knew that no matter how much it hurt or what we lost, I had to get through to you. And believe me, if it wasn't for the Lord's strength, I would have ran out of there like all the other times. But, I couldn't move."

"I'm glad it happened." She got up and emptied her glass in the sink.

"Why? There were a lot of hurtful things said that day." I reminded her.

"Yeah, that's true, but look at us now." She came over and gave me a hug. "I love you David."

"I love you too, Sis." I returned the gesture. "Look, I have to be going." I stopped at the door. "Julie?" I asked.

"Yeah?"

"What would you have done if I was the one shooting the needles?"

"I probably would have killed you myself. But, you have enough problems of your own. With the Cerebral Palsy to be worried about, you'd better not take up 'needle pointing.'"

"That's exactly my point." I smiled.

"What is?"

"You have enough troubles of your own to deal with. Each day you begin to fight new battles of wills. Each day you make it through is a battle closer to winning the war. Why would you need the needle? Now you know why Tama, Amanda and I stayed on you like we did." I looked through the window and saw her boyfriend coming home from next door. "God bless you Sis. It isn't going to be easy. You will encounter many distractions and temptations in your walk. What goes on between you and the Lord is between you and Him. When what you do is right for Him it will feel right within you. Remember, don't be swayed."

"And what is that suppose to mean?" she urged.

"Here comes your boyfriend, 'Ole' Mr. Sponge.' I'll see you later. Take care."

I nicknamed him 'Ole' Mr. Sponge on the account that I could never remember his real name. I don't think he had a 'real' name to say the truth. The guy uses so many different aliases that I never believe it when he tells somebody his name. He reminds me of a rubber ball. He's been bounced from one jail to another. He can never make up his mind. He bounces around from place to place as often as he changes names. Instead of trying to keep it all straight I just call him 'Ole' Mr. Sponge. It fits him well.

"Howdy, David. Whatcha up to? The same-o-same-o?" He greeted me with his hand up in a high-five fashion as he passed by.

"Hey," was all I could think to say.

I moved on not returning his high-five. Ole' Mr. Sponge isn't the kind of person I like to talk to. All he talked of is where to meet the next pusher and how much to use at one time. To look at him for any real length of time gets me wondering what he was like as a child. *He must have been a homely child.* I thought as I watched him pass.

He's bony, with short grungy hair and a bush of a beard to match. His eyes hollow and deeply set. He resembles one of those wrinkly puppies. Scabs galore, colorless skin and a laugh that, like a spooked wind, would scare anyone.

What does she ever see in him?

Beauty is in the eyes of the beholder!

"Whoever finds his life will lose it, and whoever
loses his life for my sake will find it."
(Matthew 10:39, NIV)

SAME OLD STORY

Chapter Nine

I hadn't felt the bond we'd build between us since my little man was brought home from the hospital. It was definitely stronger now, compared to then, the first time I'd held my first-born.

If I had held my son in my arms that night, believing in history repeating itself, it would not have been possible. The father-son bond I dreamed of was forever going to be weakened, if not broken, by the miles placed between us.

Life for me was plagued by my father's wrong doings. I vowed not to do what my father had done some ten or fifteen years ago. However, fate was not in my control.

No! No more. Not again. I thought.

Tears swelled in my eyes as I held my tiny son's body in my arms. My legs trembled and my whole being shook at the thought of living life without my child.

How will I ever explain this to you? Will you understand? I pray that you will forgive me. But, at this point in life, little man, I think I'd understand if you grew up to hate me as I did your grandfather. God, I hope not.

Holding my eight month old to my chest, I savored and recorded into memory ever sound and movement Joshua David made. His tiny heart beating largely against my chest.

This is too much. It is too damned hard to cram a lifetime of father and son happiness into a few hours. Eight months is just too short. I want to watch you grow, laugh and cry. I want to be there and love you, the way a daddy should.

As a young boy, my own father did this very thing to me. How could Ross do it? Was he so care-less? So caught up in himself that it was easier to duck out on his responsibilities? Or, was it because I was born with Cerebral Palsy? (Which is a paralysis affecting the ability to control movement that is caused by brain lesions resulting in prenatal defect at birth). Ross only knew the reason himself…and they went to the grave with him.

When Joshua was born, all I thought of was being the best daddy a child could want despite my limitations. I never dreamed that I'd ever be in my father's shoes. Not by choice anyway. Gina left the house earlier, claiming she didn't want to see her husband go. It was hard for me to believe that, considering she threw me out. She had her reason. That was made crystal clear. I didn't blame her for doing it, yet at the same time, I never thought this day would come. Our marriage could have been better and lasted forever.

What went wrong?

Friends and family warned me. Saying that Gina didn't know what she wanted out of life. What she wanted was the recognition of being seventeen and married. If Gina was in love, she didn't act it.

I, on the other hand, was lost in love with her. The signs were unseen. All I ever wanted was to be the best husband and father possible. Gina would be proud to be Mrs. David Brian Rossman.

The saying was true. Love is blind. Watch out, the awakening is frightening. A nightmare.

Someone wake me up.

Reluctantly, putting Joshua in his playpen, I went to the bedroom I shared with my wife and started packing, pulling the blue nylon duffel bag out of the closet and folding all the clothes that would fit. I grabbed a baby wipe container full of pictures, my Bible, a copy of "This Present Darkness" and all the Christian cassette tapes I owned, stuffing all these things into the duffel bag as well. *It's hard to believe that my life has been reduced to a duffel bag.*

I placed the bag at the end of the bed and folded the fuzzy yellow racecar blanket that my father, Ross had given to me one year when I was a kid. That was the last thing I'd received from him.

Why couldn't he have given me his love in place of material things? Didn't he know that the love of a son couldn't be bought?

Had Ross ever told me that he loved me? Not that I could remember. How sad.

"David," came a voice from the hallway. "Don't you want to spend time with J.D. before you go?"

Peering over to my mother-in-law with tears forming in our eyes. "No. It would be best for the both of us if I just left. I have to break the bond that I've built. I can't handle the idea of leaving him. If I stay close to him now, it will be that much harder."

"He's your son, David. Go spend time with him while you can." Sue's voice cracked.

No response. I picked everything up and headed for the hallway. Sue reached out with her motherly arms, grabbing me about the neck, pulling me in and sobbed.

This is too much. I can't handle this.

Like the walls of Jericho, my fortress was conquered. Tears fell to their death on the ground, like the people of that city. No trumpets sounded here.

"I wish there was something I could say or do to keep you here. We love you, David. Charles and I have always treated you like our son." She added.

"I know. In some ways, I've felt more love from the two of you than I got from my own parents...in others, I didn't." I paused for a moment. "I really felt like a part of the family when you and Charles tried to smooth out our fights or when you gave us room so we wouldn't feel smothered. Don't get me wrong. I appreciate everything you've done. But, to be honest, if you both would have quit treating her like a helpless child and showed her how to be independent and responsible, then she may have been ready for marriage. If you could have shown her that you'd be here if she needed you, but you weren't going to hold her hand throughout her life, maybe this wouldn't be happening."

Sue pushed away slowly. "What are you saying?"

"You've done more harm than good." I moved away. The hallway fell silent. Ice daggers pierced my flesh from behind.

Placing the stuff next to the front door along with the picture of J.D. at six months that Gina had given me, I stood there, wondering if death was easier to deal with. Even a slow death would be better than what was about to happen.

"David, come in here and see your son before you leave."

I did as I was told and took a seat on the couch in the living room. "Can I hold him?"

"Of course, David, he's your son. Spend all the time you can." Charles handed over the sleeping child. "Is there anything we can do to change your mind about leaving?" He waited.

The words were heard but there was no response.

"You know, Sue and I could have thrown in the towel several times. But, we didn't. We stayed and worked things out." Charles went on.

"Well, I'd love to stay and work things out. But, Gina has made her decision and I made the mistake. The only one who can help now is God." I tightened my hold on J.D.

Charles left the room.

This sad daddy stared at the bundle of joy asleep in my arms...for the last time. Those small fingers wrapped around a forefinger, those delicate muscles and tendons, those fingernails.

My gaze moved down to J.D.'s feet, tracing his toes with a gentle hand.

I can't believe God blessed us with this little miracle. I thank God everyday for the gift of your life.

I moved my hands from his feet to his hands, then his head, running my hand over the baldness. Tracing the blond eyebrows and lashes. My son, our son, was perfect.

The baby stretched, his hands reaching for the air, his mouth opening wide. Oxygen filled the brain. The bluish-gray windows to his soul looked up at me with hope and innocence. Again, I wondered if my son would ever understand or if he was going to hate me.

Time was precious and short. I wanted to freeze this moment forever. I was happy holding my son. My happiness shattered...

A knock at the door...the end had arrived!

I saw my life pass before me. My son would not know me. He wasn't going to want to know the man who had left him. Fright swelled in my gut.

NO! Not yet! I don't want to let him go.

"Hi Cousin." I said softly while locking in on her crystal blue eyes with my hazel ones.

Is there really a new hope and life out there, like your eyes tell me there is?

"This is Sue, my mother-in-law. And this..." holding J.D. up for her to hold, "...is Joshua David." I smiled proudly. Tears formed in my eyes.

"Oh, he's adorable. He's so cute." As she took him into

her arms, his small eyes peered up at her as if to say, "Who the heck are you?"

Charles stood at my right, Sue at my left. The heat in the house was rising. Temperatures building and tension mounted.

"He's a really good boy. They were lucky." Sue pointed out, this reminding me of the obvious.

Like I don't feel bad enough at this moment.

"Oh yeah, I know. He seems very alert." Nini commented with a smile.

Glancing around the room, avoiding the end and trying to retain everything I had seen in this house. The freshly painted white walls complimented the new gray-blue carpet. The photo of Gina and I just six months before we were married hung to the right of the fireplace.

Would that be here the next time I'm here? Will I ever come back?

Gina's 'Employee of the Month' photo from Taco Bell hung to the left. She looked great. The oversize pink turtleneck and the new short haircut fashioned around her face brought out the warmth in her almond shaped brown eyes.

Well, Sweetness, if this is what you've always wanted and Daddy's little Princess always gets her way, one way or another, you got it. I hope you'll be happy raising our son alone. I'll be dying with every day that passes. One thing is for certain. I still and always will love you.

Sue's precious bell cabinets, filled with bells from everywhere were all different. My favorite was the one on the center shelf, the rose-colored crystal one with a frosted picture of Disneyland on the front. In the back was the engraving, 'June 16, 1990.'

That was the best week of my life. Why did we have to return here... to this house?

Having seen everything, I glanced down the hall towards Charles and Sue's bedroom. The dogs were barking. They needed out.

Time to go.

"Come here, Son." I reached out with trembling arms as the tears surfaced. "I love you J.D." hugging him like a snail to a window, not wanting to let go.

"Are you ready, David?" Nini asked gingerly, knowing that this wasn't easy.

I nodded.

"Okay, J.D., it's time to go to Grandma." Kissing him one last time as I handed him to his Grandmother.

"Sue, take care of him for me." Tears were coming, I couldn't talk, my throat was closing and I couldn't breathe. *I have to get out of here.* "Be a good boy for Grandma, Pa and Mommy. I love you J.D."

"I will, you know that. We'll send pictures when we get them." Sue agreed.

Turning towards the door…

I lost it. I could barely walk. Nini took one arm, Charles the other. Together we made it out the door. I felt like the boy in the bubble. Taking those first breaths of life outside those once confined quarters. I was free, in a way, and yet, they were holding a corpse.

"You help him, will you?" Charles asked Nini.

"Sure. He'll be fine, he just needs time."

Managing to get my balance as Charles outstretched his hand, I shook it. "Son, don't worry, things will work out."

"Remember, absence makes the heart grow fonder, and with words you'll just have to write Gina letters that will make her fall in love with you again." Sue yelled from the front room.

Yeah right. Like that's the only thing that will save my marriage.

TAILLIGHTS

Chapter Ten

Ever think of life as a car? Driving from one destination to the other, trying to get things done and always in a rush. Look in the rearview mirror and what is seen? Jesus is standing there waving slowly as we drive off. Is He crying because we won't want to stop and see what life has for us? Is He asking us to come back or just waving us on? Driven by pride and 'self', we continue on. Yet, Jesus stands there watching for us as our taillights fade in the darkness.

As a child, I remember watching as my earthly father drove away from his family and his responsibilities. He and my mother had their reasons for not staying together, but never did I think it would stop me from knowing my father. I hardly saw my father after that. I wondered if he was sad about leaving or relieved as I watched his taillights fade in the night.

As a young father, separating from my then wife due to 'irreconcilable differences' was tough. After several months of being apart, we would talk about getting back together. I went to visit her and our son one evening. We talked of where we were going in life. She was pregnant with our second child and our son was nearing two years old. We both wanted to get back together, but we couldn't agree on that at the same time. Either she wanted me back when I wasn't ready or vice versa. Either way, it ended up we would remain friends.

I drove off that night with my pregnant soon-to-be ex-wife and our son waving at me in the rearview mirror. I cried the whole way home. There were a few times when I wanted to stop and turn the car around, but driven by 'I have to find myself', holding on to pride and needing most of all to find God, I drove into the night.

I cried tears of sadness and my heart cried tears of pain. I knew deep inside that things would work out. Never did I think that I'd never see my children again.

Now, remarried and starting over again, my ex has gone on with her life, as I have. One Sunday morning as I left for church, my daughter popped up in her bedroom window and cried as she yelled for me to stay home with her and Mommy. I saw her sad eyes and felt my heart longing to hold her but the desire to get to church and be in the presence of God was stronger. I cried all the way to church with her voice echoing in my ear.

Today, I not only slow down to enjoy the people the Lord put in my life, when I go places, I ask the Lord to go with me in the car and not stay behind waving in the rearview mirror.

Let people see the light of Jesus and not the glow of your taillights.

LIFE FOUND IN A MOMENT

Chapter Eleven

Is depression a genetic disorder passed down from generation to generation? Or is depression one large demon in Satan's army, with arms long enough to embrace all who are not strong enough to fight it?

Depression almost got me a few times and has just recently tried to re-enter. I know suicide isn't the way out. It wasn't six years ago and it isn't now.

August 9, 1994

After the divorce from my first wife, the thought of never seeing my two sons was more than I could take. As much as I wanted to rebuild my life and make a go of being single again, I found myself in the company of depression and it's 'happy to do me in" adversary, the box knife.

Several months of working graveyard and missing my children, I finally gave in to the lullabies of death and the warmth of feeling no more pain.

9 AM on the morning of August 9th, my arm became the sheath for a blade. In that instance, no pain was felt, just the sound of 'paper being torn' as the blade left a seven-inch reminder down my right arm. No blood was seen. No cries heard. Within, I thought I'd done the job, but You, Lord sent Your angels out to help. Two co-workers rushed to my side and held me up. Clutching my arm with a clamp like grip above my head. When people asked "Why?" All I could say was, "I'll do it again."

On the way to the hospital, I spoke of Jesus and Satan and the battle going on for my soul. It sounded good to me and yet, inside, I didn't care one way or the other. It was a 'winner takes all battle'. I was tired of the fight and thought; *if I live, I've lost everything already. So, who the heck cares if I die?*

Once at the hospital, I spoke with the doctor about the different voices I heard. You know, the ones that tell you that you're doing right when you're really not. The doc left the room and for the first time, I saw the damage that I did to myself. Flesh folding back exposing the tendons and veins. Still, there was no pain but the sight made it all real.

Wow!!! I actually did what I said I'd never do. Try to take my life with a box knife in my right arm. How dumb! How stupid!! How lost!!!

There, as I lay on the table beneath a large lamp, I heard His voice. There was and is no mistake in that.

"My son, why did you do this? I didn't ask you to do this."

Then and there I began to feel the pain. Not the pain from my self inflicted death but the pain Jesus felt when the nails went in. The pain He felt for the world. The pain He felt for me. But unlike He, who knew His course in life was to die so that a world of strangers could live, I WANTED to live. Not just for myself, but my children and for the Lord. He kept me from certain death.

I've always remembered that someone told me where to find the knife and exactly how to cut myself just right. I've learned through survival that you NEVER help in that way.

If there is ever anyone contemplating suicide and the warning signs are seen, listen to the person. Don't just say "It's your loss. It's your life." Try to help talk them out of it any way possible. Remember, the people wanting to kill themselves are just crying out. Christ died so that we didn't have to. He gave His life so that we could have ours.

Celebrate life.   Celebrate Jesus!

PATHS THAT CROSS
Chapter Twelve

I wonder why You place us where we are in life. Is it because You want us to meet people? Or know the true weight of loneliness, to bond with our companion? To bond with You as never before? Knowing You in a way that should others want to be in our lives, it isn't us at all they want to be around, but rather You.

Life is just that...Life, a gift given to us by You. Will our lives turn out the way You planned? In the end, that answer is yes, for You know the ending already. I pray that Your endings and our endings are the same.

Why is it that people walk into our lives only to vanish as fast? There are times when I feel like I've become part of the woodwork again. I'm seen but now saw. I talk but no one listens. They glance rapidly as they move on in another direction. Am I no longer wearing Your face? Is my countenance wrong?

I know what is meant by 'paths that cross', but I have a hard time dealing with the moment afterwards, when it's time to move on. If I've wronged anyone during my walk with You, I'm sorry. Do I try too hard to do things the right way? Do I hang on too tightly to people and things? I don't want to push my friends away. Yet, I do it all the time.

I'm thankful that You are constant and that we are friends.

HOW CHRIST MOVED

Chapter Thirteen

For years I stood at the door to my life. Not just any door, a revolving door. Every time I look down that narrow road to what I dream to be my future, I remember the past. I pray the visions on the horizon come true. I hunger to help others. Seeing smiles and hearing the laughter of freedom.

I understand the words we speak and the actions we make at any given moment set the pattern for our future. I want to come and go as I please. "Give what is needed and not just the little that I have."

Three years in a row, I wanted to attend Promise Keepers. I missed it every time. I could barely get the bills paid. I had no business thinking about "PK" or any other doorway out of the dreary life that I live. I am thankful for my wife and daughter, also for the two sons I no longer see. Maybe I deserved this lifeless existence, but those whom I love deserve far more. I needed to know myself, find me somewhere inside the reflection in the mirror.

This year, 1998, our pastor talked about "The Summit" with Dr. Cole, author of Maximized Manhood and Christian Men's Network meeting in Seattle, WA. An open invitation was given to the men of our church.

I would love to go to the Christian Men's Network. It would be a work of God Himself to open the door. I thought as I sat next to my wife in the pew.

"You're going." Donna said.

"Right. It's a few weeks away, but not enough time for me to ask for the time off from work. We can't afford it anyhow."

"Just trust Him. He'll make the way."

Sure, I thought. "Okay."

One Saturday morning I stepped out in faith while attending a men's meeting at our church.

"Gary, here's the money for a ticket to The Summit." I smiled as I let go of the only cash I had for the week.

"Great. You'll love it." He assured me.

As the meeting drew nearer, my wife Donna, our roommate Sylvia and I began to really pray about my going to Seattle. The more we prayed, doubt wanted to stay attached to my brain.

"I don't have the cash to stay there for the whole event and our car won't make it there and back every day. Rent is due and I can't get the time off."

"Oh, ye of little faith." Sylvia said.

"Just trust Him and things will work out." Donna reminded me.

That day at work I began to see things fall into place.

"David, I've given you these days off so you can go to that church thing." My boss informed me.

"You're prayers have been answered." A co-worker stated with a smile. "You'd better be there too, my friend."

"I will." I said.

I hope.

The next Wednesday night, church was nearly empty. The meetings were on Thursday, Friday, and Saturday.

We were standing in the third pew from the front singing songs and loving the Lord.

"Go greet someone." Pastor urged.

Everyone was hugging someone.

"Here David. This is spending money for you." A man said as he shook my hand.

"Thanks…" my voice trailed off as I fell back into the pew. My eyes filled with tears as I held fifty dollars in my hand.

I looked at my wife. She smiled. The Lord was making Himself real to me and she knew it.

"Hey David." I felt a hand on my shoulder.

"What's up, Brad?"

"I can't afford to stay in Seattle so Dale and I are driving back and forth in his car. I'll pick you up and we'll meet Dale here at the church every morning."

"That would be great, thanks."

I'm actually going to Seattle.

Dr. Cole taught on being Paymasters, Kings, Priests and living up to our names. We heard testimonies and worshipped the Lord. It was great!

Dr. Cole said, "At the end of this weekend everyone here will have to give a one minute testimony about what happened to you here."

I hate getting up in front of people.

I decided not to be controlled by fear, but rather, step up to the challenge and move to the next level in my faith.

I hardly got any sleep those three days. When I got home later that night, Donna and Sylvia were waiting to hear what was going on. I told them of the items available to purchase. I needed about $100. All I had was $27. By the time I went to sleep, it was time to get up and leave again.

Day Two. More testimonies were given and more friends

were made. I cried when I heard how to stop generational curses and the iniquities of a father from being passed on to the generations coming up.

Dr. Cole asked for an offering for the Christian Men's Network so he could continue to reach men all over the world. I still had the $27.

I wanted to get Donna a shirt if nothing else. I wanted to give to the ministry too. What was I to do?

I held the money in my hands and prayed that the Father's will be done. I gave to the offering. I didn't go to lunch that day. I stayed in the room and worked on a poem.

Giving in the offering felt like the right thing to do. Quietly I prayed when a young lady touched my hand. Surprised that she was there at all, I looked in her eyes. She was crying very hard.

"David, it helps me to see you seeking the Lord with all your heart. The Lord told me to give this to you." She placed in my hand $100.

"I can't take this." I said between tears.

"Yes, you can. And do with it what the Lord would want you to do."

This young lady left as fast as she had arrived.

Thank you Father God. Now I can get those tapes and share them with Donna. I thought.

At the very second I felt a check in my heart.

Father, I prayed. *I repent right now for the selfish thoughts that I just had. I ask for your forgiveness. Please help me to be a good steward with the money that you've given to me. Amen.*

I noticed a young man to my left across the room. He and his wife were about to leave. With great joy, I placed an envelope on the table with his name on it and returned to my seat.

Upon leaving that day, this young man came to me, gave me a hug and said, "You gave me that didn't you?"

"Let's just say that I was told you needed it more than I do. Besides that, I care about you two." I shook his hand. He gave me a bear hug.

Third day was Saturday. I had to face the fear and give my testimony. I read my poem:

WHERE THE MEN GATHER

In a place above a mountaintop
Where the Spirit of God will not be stopped.
Learning the lesson, Becoming real men—Godly men
Living the life we are within.
The power and strength, the knowledge given
Everything received in places unseen.
Glory to the King, Praising God
For all He's done.
Focusing on the Holy One

Loving Him with worship and song
Being lifted to a higher level
No longer left to wonder why
Climbing up as one man, coming down as another
I've climbed that climb; I've reached the top
His teachings begin here
Where the men gather---
At the SUMMIT!

The end of the last day was upon us. Looking at the sales table, I thought, *sorry Babe. Couldn't get you the shirt you wanted.* I stuck my hands in my pocket and felt a piece of paper. I pulled it out.

Wow. Ten dollars! Where did this come from? Now I can get that shirt.

John Locher III approached me. "David, wait up." I shook his hand. With the other hand he gave me a folded piece of paper. "Be a good steward. Be blessed."

Thanking him, I placed the paper into my Maximized Manhood book then got into Dale's car.

On the way home, I opened the book. It wasn't just a piece of paper; it was a check for $600.

PRAISE GOD!

The rent got paid. We bought food and gave some of the money away. That night there was another T-shirt in my bag with a card signed…Be Blessed, Dale

Sunday, the young couple was at church. The man

started laughing and praising the Lord, he fell to the floor, waving an opened envelope. Tears of joy streamed down his face! I wasn't the only one God was touching and becoming real to.

A CHRISTMAS TO REMEMBER
Chapter Fourteen

Mid November, 1999. It was like a formed habit, but through no fault of my own. Hours were cut back at work and I was late with the rent. One afternoon a customer handed me a Christmas card.

"Thank you." I said with a smile and placed the card below my register.

"Don't leave that alone. Don't let it out of your sight." He instructed.

"Okay." I folded the card and pushed it into my pocket. As my break time approached, I felt my pocket to make sure the card was still there. I went up and sat at the table. I pulled the card out, unfolded it and opened it.

I began praising the Lord right then and there. In my hand I held $200.00. WOW! "Thank you, Jesus." That is what we were short on the rent. *GOD IS GOOD!!!*

Monday, December 13th, 1999, Pastor Oliver and Chad entered the grocery store where I am employed as a grocery checker. Carole Murphy and I were working together. I don't think Pastor or Chad knew how the day was going to turn out, but we were going to find out.

There are two sides to every story…

SIDE ONE:

I went to the bank that morning before work, to get some money for Donna to go shopping with. I went to work like any other day with the money in my pocket. I went to lunch at 3pm and was feeling good about the day and life in general. I purchased my lunch and went to the break-room upstairs. After eating lunch I took my usual nap. I returned to work at four. At 8pm I noticed that the fifty dollars was missing! In typical human nature, I FREAKED!!!

I traced my steps as I left the store and wondered, *"Where could it be?"* I prayed that it would show up and that whoever found it would be honest enough to return it. I prayed they would be blessed anyhow.

Upon getting home, I blew up, as this man does. Everything was whacked out of control. I had lost it. I couldn't hold on to anything and this just proves it… life at that moment was going downhill fast. I knew that the Lord would pick me up when I hit bottom. I apologized to Donna for losing her

Christmas gift money.

"Well, Honey, the person who found it probably needs it more than we do."

"Yeah, right." I said. I went to bed and prayed again that the money would show up or be in the hands of someone who truly needed it. I felt a peace come over me with the gentle words, "It will be okay!"

A co-worker asked me if I had done all my shopping yet. I replied, "No. I lost the money, but things will be fine."

SIDE TWO: Carole's Story

It was Monday afternoon. I went upstairs to the employee break-room to clock back in after my half-hour lunch from 4-4:30pm. There it was, a fifty-dollar bill lying on the floor. I picked it up, and with mixed emotions thought, "Wow, a fifty. It must belong to someone who works here. What do I do?" Sarah North, a co-worker, was at the table. "Is that a fifty?" She asked.

"Yes, it is." I said. Before anything else could be said, I walked into the manager's office and showed it to him. I explained that I just found it on the floor.

"You're kidding?" he said.

""No, I'm not kidding." We walked into the break-room and looked around as if we would find the answer.

"What should we do?" the manager asked.

"It's your call, John. You're the manager."

"Why don't you hold onto it? You found it. I'd say it's yours."

Another burst of mixed emotions hit me as I thought of how I could use an extra fifty dollars, especially during the holidays. But, I knew it belonged to someone here at work and I couldn't just pocket it even though I was given the opportunity.

"I have an idea." I said. "Put it in an envelope with my name on it. If within a week, no one claims it, then I'll think of it as a Christmas bonus, ok?"

"Okay." John agreed.

Still swimming in the excitement about the situation, I called John on the intercom and asked if I could request a personal "thank you" from the one who claims the money. Just anyone could have said they lost it and claimed it and then the cash would have been absorbed by the store. I felt as if I had a good backup for wanting to make sure the right person got the money and not just 'anybody' got it.

The next day I enjoyed off. Wednesday it was back to the grind. Curiosity had me but I paid little mind to it. I was helping David with a customer's groceries when he asked if I remembered that day Pastor Oliver was in the store.

"Yeah," I replied.

"I lost fifty bucks that day."

I'm sure my eyes enlarged two sized as I said, "David, guess what? I found it."

He was excited. I was excited to tell him the story of finding it. He was so impressed in fact that after a short pause he whispered, "Keep it."

"Donna and I prayed about it and were at peace with it being gone, hoping it was found by someone who needed it more than us. I just want to say thank you for returning it to me. Not to many people would be honest enough to do that with that amount of money. You deserve it."

I, too, had prayed about it hoping that if God wanted me to have it, I would. I thanked David with tears in my eyes and felt totally blessed.

I guess the moral of this story is, that honesty does pay and money really isn't as important as some people's morals.

I still haven't figured out the connection of Pastor being in the store and David losing the money that same day...Just wanted to share the story.

Thanks, David.   ---Carole

Carole,

I truly think there is no connection to the story and Pastor shopping at the store. I think the connection was one even

Greater than Pastor Oliver. We were tested and I believe we passed. I was blessed far more than you can imagine...Merry Christmas.   ---David

A day or so later another customer came through my line and handed me fifty dollars.

"Wow. What's that for?" I asked

"I was told to give this to you. When he tells you to do something, you obey and that is what I'm doing. May your Christmas be blessed."

"It is." I smiled again as he left the store.

As Christmas Eve drew closer, gifts began to arrive at the store and the apartment from customers and co-workers alike.

Christmas 1999 will definitely be a Christmas to remember!

SOUNDING BOARD

Chapter Fifteen

I wanted to thank you for the many blessings that I have received from you this past year. Not just for the material things, but also for the simple things: a kind wave from a stranger, caring smiles from a friend. The simple "I love you" that I got from loved ones. These things mean a lot to me.

I wanted also to be honest with you and get some things off my chest. I don't want you to feel like a dumping ground thus having to feel the weight of my problems as I do. So, as I write this, I will think of you as a duck. Anything and everything I say, you may hear and also let roll off your back.

My wife and I went to a New Years' Eve get together at our church. I saw many friends there and even said 'hello' to a few of them. I wanted so much to get filled with the excitement of the evening and enjoy life at that moment. Yet, I couldn't. As my wife chased our daughter about the room I watched everything that was going on. The basketball playing, the little boy smacking the purple balloon with a ping pong paddle. I began to wonder why it is that I never got to enjoy those interactive simple things. Even as a child I had to settle for the sidelines. I wish I could be carefree now as my daughter was the night of the party, running about without a worry, even though the watchful eyes of her father saw her and her mother close behind her.

I found myself alienating myself from the world and the friends I have come to make around me. I want to be more open with them and enjoy them more, yet as the days pass, I see myself no longer doing the things a father and husband should do. Except like a robot. I am programmed to provide for my family, not just out of love, but because it is what the man does. I work each day on sore feet that no longer want to hold me up. I work all the time and for what, to pay the bills that never seem to get caught up. I come home and find things to fuss and bicker about. I vent my frustrations by yelling at my wife and wanting her to do more.

Hugging my daughter just before she runs off to bed at night and saying a prayer with her is a blessing, still it is just a moment that passes so that life, as I know it can move on. I cannot stop and take life's enjoyments in to the fullness that I know is intended for me to do. I read scripture at night before slipping off to dreamland but wake with thoughts of what will happen the next day. Will I get lunch today? Will this bill get paid? Will all the needs of my family get met today? Will I be able to stay out of the way of the negative and stay in the positive? Will I be able to stand on my feet for one more day?

In the past few months, I've pulled away from friends. I've enjoyed them from afar. Wanting to embrace them and tell them how much I care, but staying away from them for fear of hurting them. I love many people and care for them so much. I want the world for them, but have this great fear that if they know me too long and get too close, their lives will shatter and I will be the one throwing the bomb. I know I shouldn't feel this way, yet I do.

In May 1998, while at church, Linda, a youth Pastor had a vision for me. "There is a snowball effect happening to you. And that snowball is getting larger and larger, until it breaks."

Today, January 17, 2000, as I was turning into the parking lot at work, I was involved in a fender bender with another vehicle. All seemed well as I walked into the store, but in the time it took me to go upstairs to the break-room and put my lunch in the refrigerator, the whole ordeal hit me like a brick. WHACK!!!

I lost all composure and had to leave work. Upon getting

home and talking to my wife, we sat in the bedroom and cried together. "When will this snowball stop rolling at me and then stop all together?" In the last two months, I've realized that I am in the center of the snowball, heading head over heels. My whole being is really tired of the confusion and hard times. My heart can't take the pain anymore. It aches at the thought of not helping others. Giving is what I was meant to do yet, how does a person give when there isn't anything to give?

In the words of my good friend, Karen, 'How can you shelter the homeless and feed the hungry when you are the homeless and hungry?' Karen gave me some scripture to look up: 2 Samuel 5:20, Isaiah 40:31 and Isaiah 41:15. Then Sylvia called and prayed for me. 'Speak Mountaineze, David. This is a good time to speak mountaineze and carry your family through to victory. Your battle has already been won by Jesus Christ.'

In the last few hours since this morning's fender bender, I've encased myself in praying in the Spirit, reading the Word and listening to Christian Music. Within all this, I've come to the clear understanding that no matter how dark the road is we travel, if we believe and seek the Light, His love is good and strong. The stone that was rolled away some 2000 years ago will be my cornerstone...even now.

OUR PLANS B AND C ARE NOT HIS PLAN A
Chapter Sixteen

April 1, 2000 - The men's breakfast was at church this morning. I told my wife all week that I wasn't going. All she would say is, "Yes you are. There's no excuse. You're off work. You are going." Then she'd smile and tell me she loved me. I'd only been to two previous 'Men's breakfast' due to working or just plain laziness. None of the reasons mattered now, I was going to this one. And I was expecting something. Would it be an encounter with Christ or just a word of knowledge? Both of these reasons were good reasons, but as I woke up this morning, all I thought of was the food. *I am a hungry man, Lord.* I thought to myself. Then I heard *'I would give you more than food'*. I knew as I drove from Lacey to Yelm, that God was going to show up and He wanted to give me something. What it was I wasn't sure of, but if He wanted to give, I was open to receive.

After praise, prayer and talking over steak and eggs, the message for me was clear. Faith has a voice, truth has a sound and change isn't change until it changes. I have to die daily to myself and grab hold of the vision for the future of my family, because a man without a vision will always return to his past. During closing prayer I prayed, *Father God, for the last few months I've been a wishy-washy man. As this move to Idaho draws near, I am still undecided. I believe that You've opened the door and that you will make a way. I know I need to trust You, yet I find myself questioning how. The house is there waiting, the job has ended here. But the money, Lord, where is it coming from? Lord, I don't want to be a man lost in the tide of life or a leaf that gets tossed to and fro by the wind. I want to be a faithful and trusting man. Please show me, Lord. Tell me what it is I have to do so that I can understand what it is You want me to do. I ask this in Jesus' name, Amen*

April 2, 2000

I went to church alone. Not knowing what to expect but at the same time expecting something. All the way there I prayed that I would get a clear answer about this move to Idaho. An answer that I KNEW was from Him and not my own mind. I understand that when a child of God tries to move in his own flesh, Satan will move in to steal, kill and destroy what it is we have or strive for. I didn't want the prince of darkness moving my family and then killing us off like sheep to the slaughter. I believe that our God, my God, is going to take us where He wants us. In the end of this trial, there will be another victory in Jesus!

As the service drew near and my faith wrestled within, my flesh took over. "Yes, I know that the Lord wants us to go, but the house is going to be dozed over if it isn't rented and there's the issue of the money to get there. The apartment is packed, but we haven't got the money to move on." I told a friend.

"You are being a wishy-washy person, David. Don't worry about it. If you truly got a word from the Lord, go on that word and trust in Him. He will keep you. I believe you should go."

I knew all that I was hearing was true, yet I still couldn't settle the matter within myself.

Shortly after Praise and Worship started, I sat in my seat and wept. I couldn't control the tears. I softly sang the words to the song as tears fell to the floor. "...I give you my heart, I give you my soul... Every breath that I take, every moment I'm awake, Lord do your will in me."

I couldn't stop the waterworks. A friend laid hands on me, prayed for my spirit to get at peace then he prayed for the healing of Cerebral Palsy. I cried harder. As I rocked back and forth in the chair, I praised the Lord for everything that He was doing. I wanted direction and He was giving it to me. My life isn't mine but His. I didn't want to control it anymore. I didn't want to move without His prompting.

I thought of asking Pastor for prayer about this move after church, but no sooner had I thought of it, the pastor said, "If you come up here and ask for prayer so that you can get an answer from God about something that is going on in your life, I will tell you to get on your face right now for an hour. Then I'll ask you what the Lord told you."

Well, forget going up there. I said to myself. *Why not just get on my face before God and wait for the answer?*

Pastor began the service with Isaiah 62:10. When I read it, the words spoke to my heart and my heart leaped within my chest. I knew we were going to Idaho. Yet, I still wasn't sure about the money thing. "$1,500.00 is a lot to get together in a short time. I believe that we were to jump now. Go now. Something wasn't right.

Upon getting home, I showed my wife the verse that had touched my heart. She read it and said the same thing. Then I called my friend and Spiritual father and again brought up the subject of Idaho.

"We are going, just not right now. We were suppose to leave on April 18th, but we've decided to go for a visit then and see what's what there."

"Okay, how much money do you need to get there for the visit?"

"$400.00. We're going with Donna's parents so we have to pay for part of the gas and hotel stays and things like that."

"Put out a fleece. Trust the Lord that you will have the $400.00 at that time. It all is according to your faith."

We went to church again that evening. The message was about how we as humans tend to jump in the flesh to fix a God given plan. Our plans B and C all the way through Z, isn't going to be His plan A for our lives. How can we get through life trying to do things we're not supposed to do and trying to be people we're not?

"If God gives you a plan, go with it, don't try to fix it yourself." The speaker said.

She gave the scripture, Genesis 31:3, and upon reading this, Lu, Donna and I started laughing.

We knew that we knew that the Lord was going to bring us home when we were finished in Idaho.

Joanne asked, "Is anyone in here that was given a plan from God, but you're trying to work it out yourself? I want you to come up here to the front and I want to pray for you."

I looked at my wife and asked if she was going to go up with me, but I didn't wait for her. I knew I was going up.

I stood there and praised the Lord for all that He had done. Joanne prayed for us. I felt as though I was going to fall. I was rocking on my feet. There was a warm feeling on the back of my neck, like a hand was holding me there, but it wasn't a human's hand. Not one person could hold me like this and be loving and warm. At times, I felt like I was swaying in circles. Then, POOF...down I went.

I lay on the floor, shivering and shaking, yet I couldn't get up. I wasn't sure how long I was down there, but I knew when I got up, that the money would be there and that WE were going to Idaho.

I returned to my seat and saw tears in my wife's eyes.

"Well?" I asked.

"We're going to Idaho." She smiled.

I know that when the Lord gives you something, take it and go with it. He will make the way clear.

"Then the Lord said to Jacob, 'Return to the Land of your fathers
and to your family, and I will be with you.'"
(Genesis 31:3)

WHEN GOD MOVES

Chapter Seventeen

The last few months as my hours at QFC have dwindled, I've had a lot of time to be with myself and renew my thoughts and look at situations differently. I've found that if I'm willing to listen and watch my family the way God intended for me to, I can see that my wife isn't only my spouse, but my partner with Christ and my best friend. My daughter isn't just my daughter, but my teacher. If I allow myself to be taught, she teaches me new things. Most of what I've learned in the last few months is that each day, we have moments with God. Times in our lives where He shows up and lets us know just how much He loves us.

I put aside my poetry for a bit to work on a collection of short stories. HIS ONLY TEAR is the name of this new project. In it, I'm attempting to put together stories that represent the moments when Christ was there for me. What I'm about to write is just one of those 'Make a memory' moments with my Lord.

I've worked for Thriftway, Stock Market, QFC, Fred Meyer and Kroger for the better part of my seven years in Washington. I've made many friends and even though it pains me to say it, I've made a few enemies. All in all, I've kept up with the times and worked as many hours as possible to make a living here.

I started out in Yelm and then most recently moved to Lacey. Hours were fine to begin with and there was nothing to worry about. Christ was going to bring me through the dark times. Hours began to fall and that was okay. I stood firm in my faith that all would work out and that Christ would and will get the glory of it all. One thing I found for sure is that there is peace in a single word.

Saturday, March 18th, I stood in my check stand at work fidgeting, in my mind, with the conversation my wife and I have had over moving out of state. Over a period of time, I would bring up moving to Texas or California. We would bicker back and forth for a bit, with the understanding that if we couldn't agree, we wouldn't move then I'd drop the idea all together. That day in the check stand, I was saying to myself, *Texas? No. California? No.* Then I prayed, God please give me direction. Take the stress of the inconsistency of hours away and bring peace into our lives. Father, I ask this in Jesus' name, Amen.

No sooner had I finished that prayer that the word *Idaho* came into mind. Idaho? I asked to myself. Then I felt a spring in my spirit. A smile appeared on my face as I gave out a whisper, "Yes!"

One thing is for sure; it must be from God's guiding hand. Doors opened up as fast as others closed. During lunch I phoned my sister, Julie in Idaho to see how she was doing. We talked about how we wanted to be closer as friends and not just brother and sister. Over the years, when Julie and I spoke, one subject came up. Jesus Christ. Again, we talked about Him, our love for him and what He does for us. We talked about my hours being cut back and that one of my bosses at work had asked me if I wanted to be laid off. I had told him no at the time. Then Julie mentioned there's an Albertson's right down the street from a two-bedroom house with a fenced in backyard. She placed a $200 deposit on this house but was uncertain about moving into it herself.

"You can move into it. The rent is only $350 per month. You can find a job here." She said without hesitation.

"Are you sure?" I started to smile.

"Yes, come on down."

"You find out for sure if it's okay that we moved into the house and if that's a go, I'll let my boss know."

"Ok. I'll call you on Monday."

We hung up the phone and called my wife at home and told her what had just happened. She agreed.

Monday came and the house is ours. I told Julie that we couldn't be there before the 18th of April, so we could tie things up here. There wasn't a problem. We just have to have the $350, for the rent when we get there. Not to mention getting there ourselves.

Where were we going to get the money for this move?

Wednesday, when I returned to work, I told my boss of my move in April.

Thursday, I phone the Albertson's over in Lacey and got the phone number to the store in Emmett, Idaho. I phoned there and spoke with the District Manager, who told me to send in my resume, and application.

Friday, I was laid off.

Saturday, March 25th, was my last day at work. By the end of that day, my boss hands me a letter of recommendation, a handshake and his best wishes.

So we are preparing for a new adventure in our lives.

In the short time that we've been members of this church family, we have been taught so much. We've loved so much and learned to trust even more. In God we trust and Him we shall follow.

I read Genesis chapter 12. In it, God told Abram to take

his family and move to the land of Canaan. As I read and re-read that over and over to my wife, I understood that He was speaking to me.

Now, like any human, I am uncertain in my mind what the outcome of this adventure in life will be, but I believe in the Lord and His protection is on my family. I trust He will not lead us to the wolves; rather, He will lead us through the darkness.

RETURN TO THE BLESSINGS

Chapter Eighteen

By now there are many of you wondering why the Rossman's are still in the area. As well you should think that, as I myself thought that very thought. But now, as I look back, I understand and see what was happening.

I remember saying to Donna, my wife, that 'Where He leads, I shall follow.' And although I felt weary about that statement at times, and unclear at the steps I was to follow in, I am glad that we did follow Him. For He has taken us out and brought us back to the place we love the most, 'home'.

We left the 17th of April to explore a new frontier. The ride there, with my in-laws was fun yet frustrating. I was packed in the very back of the mini van with the bedding. Donna and Anita Rose asleep on the center seat and Mom and Dad in the front. Most of the trip was spent sleeping and or reading. But the last leg of the trip proved to be more enlightening for me. Mom and I laughed as we entered Idaho and got lost in no man's land.

That night we sat in my sister's back yard and pushed Anita Rose in a swing. That was something I had never done before. When Julie got home from work the cows got loose and Harold, Julie's boyfriend was yelling for help as the cows ran through the front yard. Julie ran after them. I got up, not knowing what the heck I was going to do, but I followed. All the while thinking, *Dear God don't let these animals charge me.*

"What's David suppose to do?" Julie asked as she and Harold went for the gate. I stood in the center of the road wondering what I was to do if I did get charged.

"I didn't mean for David to help. Christ, he can barely stand up by himself let alone chase cows." Harold told Julie. Just then I stumbled, spooking the cows in towards the gate.

April 18th, next day I was up with the sun and wanting to find work…Anita and I spent the morning with Harold and Julie feeding the cows and horses.

Later that day, as Harold went about his business, Donna, Anita and I went for a walk to the park, and then met Julie at her work.

"Mike is next door at the store and he wants to meet you. Go on over. They need a manager over there."

I went over and met Mike. I told him of our plans to move to Idaho and that I was looking for work.

"I can only pay you $5.15 per hour. If you're anything like your sister and with the qualifications you have, you should look elsewhere with the big companies. I'd need you to start like right away."

Man, that is a cut. I'm use to getting $15.10 per hour. I thought.

"I understand that you can't pay much, but I won't turn down a job that will put a roof over my head. My only thing is that we haven't found a house to stay in. I don't want to impose on my sister any more than I have."

"Ok. You get settled and then let me know and we'll see what we can do."

That night before bed Julie, Donna and I talked it over. We were set to go see this house that Julie had told us about before we came down.

April 19th, Mike's wife came to the house and asked Julie what it was going to take for me to go to work at the store. I told Julie, "$7.per hour at 40 hours or $8.00 at 30 hours."

Agreed. *What about the house?*

Upon seeing the house, we weren't sure. It was a 2 bedroom for $350 a month, yet in order to fit any of our stuff in the house, we'd have to knock down a few walls. It was less than 700 square feet. Smaller than the apartment we live in.

"Julie, would you take it?"

"To be honest, no. It's too small even for me."

April 20th, we applied for low housing apartments as we prepared to return to Washington to finish packing.

I went to Mike and explained our plans.

"Sounds good. If things work out and you move here, we'll create a job for you."

"Great, thanks."

April 21st, we headed for Washington.

April 24th, Donna got called to work for Census 2000.

April 30th, Julie got a note from the apartments stating that we were denied the low housing. I began praying for clearer direction about what we were to do next.

May 6th, my sister-in-law gave us her Oldsmobile. I started thinking about returning to QFC. I called there and spoke with the boss.

"Sure you can come back, but I can' only give you 20 hours a week at best."

"I'll talk it over with my wife. Thanks."

I began putting resume packets together and sending them to all the stores around town and the surrounding areas. No one was hiring at that time.

I heard about a new Albertson's opening up in Spanaway.

I found out who was in charge of that location. I sent a packet to the main company in Bellevue and to the store on Canyon Road in Tacoma.

I got an interview on May 31st, at 8AM in Puyallup. I arrived early and was done by 8am and was told to stay by the phone the next day.

That night I stopped in at the QFC in Lacey and again was offered my former job back, with the 20 hour maximum. I was then told of all the people being laid off and or terminated in the last two months. I stood there, looking at my former boss and thought, *Wow, maybe there was a reason for me to leave this company when I did.*

At 3PM on June 1st, I got the call. Albertson's offered me a full time checker position, starting out at $15.50 per hour, pending a drug test on June 2nd.

That's more than I was making at QFC.

"I don't think that will be a problem. I've never used drugs." I told the lady.

"Good, that's what we wanted to hear."

I went in for the test and was told I would hear back within a week or so with the results. The new location opens June 19th. I will start with Albertson's between the end of the month and July 9th. My unemployment ends that day. Praise God for His faithful timing!!!

AND HE CALLED YOU

Chapter Nineteen

As Christians with His call on our lives, we are to share the word and lead people to Christ. Have you ever felt like you couldn't lead anyone to Salvation even though you wanted to? That was me. Every time an opportunity arose where I could have done that very thing, I'd back out and think, *no I cannot do this. I can share my testimony but that is it.*

AMBER-

We were fast friends and became fast relatives. We talked of the future and asked favors from time to time. Favors I couldn't do for my heart belong to another. Your heart too, belonged to another, my brother. Over the years we'd talk by phone or the net. I'd preach and I'd pray. The more I talked of

Jesus and His love, the further you got.

Christ moves sometimes in ways that we don't always understand. But the tests come about and boundaries are set. Satan wants us to step over the boundaries set by trust and the heart. But, all things work out to the good of those who love the Lord.

You came for a visit while my wife was away. What a joy it was to see you. Donna wasn't sure at first if it was safe to leave us together...yet, she trusted us and she trusted God to do His will.

I wanted friends to lead you to the Lord for fear that I would mess it up. I know that I'm a writer for the Lord, but a harvester of souls? Of that, I wasn't too sure of. It had been a pleasure to have you as my sister-in-law, but I wanted you as a sister in the Lord.

Friday came. You read me a story called "T'was the Night Christ came". I fell to the floor in tears. Christ spoke to me through all the tears. "The time is now. Her heart is ready". I couldn't wait any longer.

Satan had wanted this visit to ruin both our lives, but God's plan is greater. He gave you yours. We took hold of each other's hands and paraphrased Romans 10:8-10:

"If you confess with your mouth and believe in your heart that Jesus died and was raised from the dead on the third day for the forgiveness of our sins, we shall be saved." When we opened our eyes, a new Amber sat before me.

The rest of that week, God showed up and began a work in you during every moment of the day. You saw the proof and your heart and soul agreed. Life may not get easier, but you'd see things differently and walk out your faith.

KEVIN-

I couldn't have imagined ever seeing anyone from my youthful days in Texas. Not here in Washington State. Especially fifteen years after graduation.

I knew your face but couldn't fit the place. I heard your voice. That accent! A familiarity from back home, recognizing you was hard at first. You mentioned Bible school brought you here. I knew I had to talk with you. I wanted to know what God was doing in your life. Was He working in your life back then, when we knew of each other as strangers in the halls?

You weren't too sure of me either, that is, until I walked away. Then it was clear. Our memories were clear. Strange how we met here, we never talked in school, will we talk now?

God knows what He's doing and why we take the paths we do. I thank God for His loving grace and hope to talk to you more about life and the way Christ moves.

RICK-

I could feel God on you from that first day. The way you spoke of church and the love of Christ while standing in the checkout line at Albertson's. You invited me to your church. Your smile was bright and your heart sang for His glory and wanting to win souls for His Kingdom.

In the chip lane we met once again...yet another chance to hear the love of Jesus in you. Two weeks had passed since we met that first time. Now, with no restraints and a boldness that only He could give, you laid hands on me and prayed for the healing of my legs. My day had started out dark, but after that there was no blocking the light of Jesus and the power of prayer.

We shall meet again my friend, this I trust. For faith and believing in His great love for the lost souls of this world. He weaves our lives together with strands that not even satan can break.

HE IS THERE
Chapter Twenty

In the year 2000, I've come to see a new light in my life. I can no longer look at myself and allow myself to stay the same. Nor do I think that Jesus would want me to stay that way. Yes, I have come a long way in one year's time, but I've noticed that I've attached myself to something from even further in my past, and that I have to let go of. I understand that it will be very hard to do, for I am human and humans live in the flesh and for what satisfies the flesh. Yet, I've been called to step up and look back at where I once was and be thankful for that time. At the same time, look towards the future and be ready for what my Lord has in store for me.

As I worked on New Years Eve 2001, I wondered where my kids were. What my wife was doing. What my church family and friends were all doing at that moment?

I knew my daughter was in bed, I figured my wife may have been sleeping, but I prayed that my sons, Joshua and William were doing ok and still in good health. I haven't seen either of them in eight years, but we pray for them and their mother nightly and know that God is watching over them.

I've seen family members come to Christ and I've seen others run from Him. I've felt great joy in my walk with the Lord and at the same time, I've had to fight to keep that joy going.

I've met many wonderful people over the last few years and I fear I have made a few enemies, nonetheless, everyone has touched my heart in a way that no one else can.

Christ puts all of us in places where we will meet others. Even if we don't like it at the time, everything that happens is for our benefit. I laugh at the memories, cry at them, run from them and run to them all at the same time. Knowing that in the end, I will end up in His loving arms…for He has carried me through.

I've had people see me, laugh at me, thus making me laugh. I've had people bring me to tears with a simple caring glance or word. Those moments are treasures…like seeing a friend after a long time, that instant is priceless. When a child says his or her first words, or when you've led someone to the Lord, that is golden!

When you feel the Lord speaking to your heart in the

middle of the night, so you just have to pray, that is a tender moment between the Father and you. That is a moment to write about!

There have been times when I've been drawn into a friendship and then suddenly thrust outward for no known reason, thus feeling like I've wronged that person in one way or another...only to find out later that that division was Satan trying to prevent 'Godly interaction' from happening and the fear placed in my mind was from the father of lies himself.

Well guess what satan, you've been busted!! I'm not letting you have me anymore. So, in Jesus' name, take a hike!

We are to remember where we've been so that we can see just how far we've come. But we are not to be held down by the past, for our future is in Christ and He can take us anywhere. Amen?

Jesus is there, here and everywhere!

Here's to a Glorious 2000

DEVOTION'S HEARTBEAT

(A Valentine for my wife)

Chapter Twenty-One

The moment we met, I knew she was the one. My Father in Heaven had placed her here for me to love and care for. Yet I knew not her name. All I knew for sure was that she loved the Lord and His beauty shone through her. Every move she made spoke of His gentleness. The very sound from her lips sung the notes from His heart.

I have been in love before, but not like this. I'd seen marriage before, but this one was different. Though I've found similarities between the two, there is ONE solid difference, JESUS CHRIST. I loved the Lord all my life, yet I still followed my own path. Along that path I loved and lost. Saddened by the losses, I cherish the loves and now I hold tightly to the gifts that make my life a dance. For this dance is choreographed by JESUS.

True, as in all marriages, we see our dark times and there were times when I've tried to reason my way out of it. Only then did I hit walls that I thought were doorways. I expressed anger when I should have loved. I've fallen and been alone when I should have picked up and embraced.

My wife has proven many times over that she is nonetheless devoted to her Lord and thus attracting me to herself. She loves me even when I feel she should turn me loose to my own. But no, she loves me more when I hate myself. She lifts me to the top when I should be at the bottom.

"You will not be apart, until I part you. She is to help you, as you are to encourage her. Then in the both of you, people will see Me. Neither is totally perfect, but this life you have is one that fits."

'A TRUE VALENTINE'

She is the one
The one that I need
The Lord gave her to me
Within her I see
The woman she is
The knowledge she has
Is the truth within
The love that she shares
Comes from knowing Him
Caring for the children
As best as she knows how

Helping me up
When I've fallen down
Soothing the pain
When nothing else is gained
Loving her for loving me
Comes from loving each other
With His loyalty

Roses and carnations do not compare
Rainbows and sun showers do not diminish her
Crystals and diamonds, rubies and sapphires
Are merely stones
Her beauty is God given
Thus an eternal glow
No amount of money will please her
For her riches aren't of earth
But there's a room in heaven
That has been there since her birth
No rushing sounds of waterfalls
Nor even a sparrow's song
Can shatter her lasting love
For her soul sings a song no other can match
Listen…
DEVOTION'S HEARTBEAT

DOWN BUT NOT OUT

Chapter Twenty-Two

I never thought of myself as handicapped. My motto is 'I have Cerebral Palsy but it doesn't have me'. I still believe that and I'll stand by that. But I do need to realize that the CP is there and one day I will have to prepare for it.

I believe also that in the Spirit realm I have been healed, but in the flesh I have not so, I have to deal with the reality of life head on. I may have to slow down more than ever before but I will NEVER be out, nor will I ever give up the fight for others who have a disability.

About two and a half years ago, my wife Donna and I went to a couple's retreat with our church. While there, it was prophesied over me that I would write books and poetry. Thus, enforcing my lifelong belief that I will one day make a living with my writing. While at this two-day retreat I ended up with

Spinal Meningitis. After being put in the hospital and being told I was going to die, I chose to fight for life and those that I love.

I took a month off work to recover, but ended up losing my home in the process. I fought my way back to work and with the help of the friends at church we weren't homeless for long. Thank God for friends who care. I returned to work with the fire for life, but I was never the same.

On March 23rd 2000, I took a voluntary lay-off from work due to lack of hours. We thought we'd visit Idaho and maybe move there. The doors we saw opening there closed very quickly. After a week we returned to Washington. My wife worked temporarily with the Census and I was on unemployment. That too was going to run out soon.

While all these changes are coming at us, I kept up with the dream that I would be able to stop swimming against the tide and roll with life. I'd see my friends and do things I've always wanted to do with my family.

I went to work for Albertson's in June 2000. I began to see myself as a manager or store director. As always I've not let the Cerebral Palsy hinder me at all. I've attacked every opportunity with vengeance and life. I've even seen my 'Self-Published' book get put in the store and customers buying them. That right there was a dream come true, but I was paying to see my name in print. I have yet to make a living from them. The two books I have written have paid for themselves, but I'm afraid that I'll never see them in print again.

I took on writing articles for the Internet. This venture has brought joy into my life. I've seen my work touch many people all over the world. Yet, due to the increasing energy crunch that we have been feeling, I will not be able to keep my computer much longer. I cannot afford the payments and pay the cost of energy to run it. For this I am sorry.

I have been to the doctor recently and have been placed in an ankle brace to help me when I'm at work. I've been taking pain pills to lessen the discomfort. I work through all this to keep the benefits at work for my family and to keep a roof over our heads.

Donna, my wife and partner in life has tried to help out as much as possible with finding a job but has not had much luck. I would like to say that 'I am the man of the house and I should be making the money', but I'm not the man of the house. Jesus is the man in my house and all that I have belongs to Him. Thus I shall step down from that role and let Him have what is rightfully His.

I recently did something that I once thought I'd never do. I got a handicapped placard for my car. Now I can park closer than I usually do, but I feel that I've somewhat given in to the CP. I have been getting tired more than normal but refused to give in all together.

At Albertson's we are selling shamrocks for Muscular Dystrophy, $1 for the green ones and $5 for the gold ones. At first, I wasn't sure I could sell one because the first time I heard a customer say 'no' I would feel defeated. I took a deep breath and prayed that God would give me the words and strength to sell as many shamrocks as I could without being forceful. I began to blast away at selling shamrocks.

"Why are you so driven to sell so many shamrocks?" a co-worker asked.

"I have Cerebral Palsy and I've never asked for a thing that I wasn't willing to work for. I've never seen drives like this to make money for CP, so if I can't help the people with CP, then I may as well help with other causes…I just think of the kids that drives me to want to do the best I can for them."

I look at my own daughter and wanting the best for her gives me the energy and drive to look past my circumstances and work through the pain to give her the best I can. Sure, I may never own my own home, be a paid writer or work at a job where I can sit most of the time, but as long as I'm able to stand (pain or no pain) I will do my level best to stay ahead of the game. I may even be in a wheelchair again someday. But, even then, I may be down but now out.

FORSAKEN NOT

Chapter Twenty-Three

"I will never forsake you."

Seeing God work in the midst of darkness is a great joy. He can touch the heart of a friend or stranger, thus they reach out to help someone else.

The world tries to keep us in its clutches, depressed and distraught over the situation in life. Just when we lose hope and want to give into the web of oppression, a way of hope appears in the works of actions or another.

I have seen the light and felt the warmth of love from the father in Heaven. A tight handshake and a cheerful smile can brighten even the blackest of days. In a time when money is tight and belts have to be pulled in, the actions of a friend can make you breathe easier.

Shortly after DOWN BUT NOT OUT was sent out, the love and grace of God began to show. Work was tense as usual; the headache pains were stronger than ever. I wanted so much to give into the moment and collapse in the check stand. How was I going to deal with the increasing energy bills and still maintain the happiness I felt every day at home? I'd been busting hump to get caught up on the bills and give my child the little things she asked for. Money has never grown on trees and dreams, though seen in the mind, are made reality with money.

Like any parent would do for his or her family, I decided to give up the computer that has helped me reach many with the stories. I couldn't continue to pay for the computer as well as the heating bills. Though the computer would have to go, my dreams of writing would have to go on the old fashion way. DOWN BUT NOT OUT was to be the last story written for the masses. Yet, that night I was reminded that my faith is not in my writing, but the Lord Jesus Christ who sacrificed His life so that those He loved could live. The loss of my computer seemed small in comparison. If He could give His life, surely I could give my computer. I'd have to rest in His arms during this time and trust that He would work things out.

The other day we received a gift of $250 from someone who had a glow in his eyes, a reassuring handshake and a smile that said, "Don't worry." In the two minutes we spoke of his up coming wedding to a very beautiful and lucky woman. In an instant my darkened day had been hit with a beam of Jesus' love and compassion.

This story is for all who look with the eyes of angels and reach out with the heart of God to help someone other than himself or herself. To all of you and especially to the couple-to-be, thank you.

As long as there are angels that walk the earth, the world will not get stuck in a slumber of despair.

GOD BLESS

FEELING THE TRUTH WITHIN AND TRUSTING IN HIM
Chapter Twenty-Four

Before I could walk, I dreamt of running. When I found out I had Cerebral Palsy, I dreamt of walking. Though I was stationary in this world, in God's realm, I was dancing rings around those who laughed at me. When I was in a wheelchair, I was a mere cripple with major problems, but in His realm, I was hell on wheels! On earth I was a loner, but to Him I was a warrior!

When I began to write poetry and stories, I was told I couldn't do it. I was told I couldn't write to pay the bills or keep food on the table. I was discouraged!

Before I accepted Christ, I got lost in circumstances of life. If things didn't go the way I thought they should, then I was doomed to fail at anything I'd ever try to be. I found the road to destruction and followed it. I wrote of what hurt and the sorrow that kills. I had the 'spoiler's touch'. Everything I did, touch or look at went belly up and stank of failure.

Listen, I may have given some people the impression that I want sympathy for having been born with Cerebral Palsy, or they may think I need praise for every 'hurdle' I jump. That isn't the case at all. God gave me the ability to write what He wants me to write. And in His timing all things will come to pass. Enjoy the good and know that when bad arrives, it will also leave, for even the bad shall be turned to the good for those who love Him. I'm not afraid to say it, "I LOVE THE LORD".

Yes, I still dream of doing lots of things. I still want to be a writer in the ranks with Dan Wooding, Nicholas Sparks, Jim LaHaye, Jerry B. Jenkins, Frank E. Peretti, Dr. Louis Cole and Dave Pelzer.

In the natural, that may seem to be a far stretch, but with Christ I may not be that far away, or I may be there already and just don't know it. One day, I'll be in their circle and touch as many hearts as they have and life will be one less struggle, but for now, I'll just seek God and let Him place me where He needs me to be.

Now, I'm not saying that I'm giving in to the world or the C.P. I'm not suggesting that anyone give up or give in to his or her handicap. Please don't get me wrong. I'm simply saying this:

"Believe in Jesus Christ as Lord and know that He will carry you through everything. You may be limited to what you can do here on earth, but in God's realm...Heaven is the limit and Heaven is limitless. If I can reach one lost person or touch one heart with my writing, then I've done my part...may the Lord bless many from the blessings I get from using the gift He gave me."

A CHOSEN GENERATION

Chapter Twenty-Five

"But you are a chosen generation, a royal priesthood,
a holy nation, His special people, that you may proclaim
the praises of Him who called you out of the
darkness and into His marvelous light."
(1Peter 2:9, NIV)

There have been times in my life when I have to re-evaluate myself. What kind of a person am I? Is life to me a costume party at which I hide behind a mask? I try to run as far as I can...I admit it; there are times when I'm not the man I want to be or should be.

I want to know Him more and I have a desire to, but the desire is stagnate. I can have all the desire in the world to know Him, but stay in a worldly slumber. I have to have the passion. When you have a passion to go after what you want, you go after it no matter what, correct? What are the signs of the passion?

Reading the Word more? Praying more? Noticing a person in need and feeling the need to help?

Yes, feeling within the hunger the way Jesus did. These are all beginnings to a hunger that can be fed but never satisfied, thus causing the passion to ignite and the flames to burn.

If I look in the mirror will I see my flesh or the reflection of Jesus coming from within? Can we step out of ourselves and help others without question or return?

I ask these questions of myself and of the readers of this story. I've looked through the eyes of the 'child needing a glass of water' and have 'the one giving the water'. I've been on both sides of the situation. I've seen the blessings that can come about.

When I get bummed about my circumstances, I think about what Jesus would do. He would try to help whomever He could in whatever way He could to see happiness in the eyes of people.

He has chosen us to help others in need. Don't be blinded by the darkness. This holiday season will see tears of joy and sadness. Heartstrings will be strummed.

Please, don't be a spectator. Get involved if you feel the need to help then do so. If you cannot, then pray. No matter how big or little the contribution...your plate of desire will be filled with the hunger and passion to see Christ. In helping a child get a toy for Christmas or a family have a Thanksgiving meal, you will feel the Lord's heart beat within your chest and see His smile appear on another person's face.

We are a chosen generation...one that can make a difference.

Be blessed this holiday season!

CRACKING THE SKY

Chapter Twenty-Six

Ever awaken in the middle of the night, wondering why you couldn't sleep? Did your eyes open suddenly looking for something or someone? Or were you awakened by the sound of yourself gasping for air as your eyes searched for a lifeline?

Last night as I slept on the couch, I was startled from my dream state by a brush on the face. My lungs expanded wide as I drew in what I thought to be my first breath of life or my final. My cat lay on the rear of the couch. Could that brush on my cheek have been the cat or the sleeve of Jesus' robe? I ran to my daughter's room to see if she was still tucked in her bed.

Jesus is coming, this I know and understand, but the hour and the day, no one knows. I feared I had missed His return and I'd been left behind.

I looked through the window to the night sky. Clear and

cool. There, far off in the distance a section of sky was lighter than the rest. I felt drawn to that oddity of the sky. Could God have been calling me to pray? Was I being shown what happens in the heavens when the children of God pray? Do prayers really crack the sky?

There have been times when I was drawn to read the word in order to find the peace to sleep. Have I stepped that far from my Father in heaven that He has to physically tough my face to get my attention? I heard Him speak clearly years back after I tried to commit suicide. My first marriage ended in divorce and I hadn't seen my two sons in a while.

"My son, I did not ask you to do this. Why would you do it?" I heard as I lay there getting sewn up.

If my Lord didn't get my attention then, He got it last night.

PRAY. Pray and you can change the world. Prayers are heard and hearts of people all over the world are being touched.

As the holidays speed toward us, I ask everyone to pray. Knowing that life can begin or end in a heartbeat, pray for family and friends and strangers alike... for paths to cross when they are meant to. Gifts were placed within you. When the time is right, that gift will be drawn out. Monday will be made. Monday will be given. Dreams will come true because of the desire placed within you. Trust the Father and not the world. The enemy is on the prowl so that he can steal, kill and destroy. The doors will be opened for you...a place made for you.

Trust the Lord, read the Word and pray.

If ever you wake in the middle of the night, pray. There is a reason you were chosen to pray at that very hour. Even the simplest prayers can make a mountain move...if only you believe. God is watching...

A war will rage in the heavens...cracking the sky!

Peace to all this holiday season...

VOICE OF THE HEART

Chapter Twenty-Seven

I know now that I'm not the man I want to be. Or the man I think that you deserve. I'm wrong, at least, on one of the statements. Yet, in the distance, beyond eyesight, there is a voice. That voice belongs to my Father in heaven.

My ears hear Him most of the time. Other times I turn the sound down. In those moments, when I'm deaf, I know that He still reaches me. I know for a fact because he gave me you.

There are times I feel wrong for you. There's more out there for you. I holler when I'm mad. Though I don't aim the madness at you, the bluntness of the words hit hard. In all honesty, in those instances, I've turned my face away from my Father and hate myself for being the man I am.

I am a dreamer: I dream of financial freedom, a big house with wooden floors and antique design, white walls and brightly lit rooms. No darkness or dreariness. I hear the sound of the ocean and children laughing. I have a passion for writing and desire to do it for a living. I'd love to see the world through my own eyes and not through the pages of a novel. Most of all I want to share it all with you.

The dreams stay in my head and never at my fingertips. A man's flesh is his own destruction. I love to make money so that I can give it away. Yet, I use what little spare cash I have to gratify the greedy man who lives in me. Flesh is a hard thing to deal with at times. I apologize for that. I understand and feel that the Lord is trying to change that part in me. I'm just too stubborn to let Him do what He wants.

I want to blame my earthly father for having died without teaching me how to be the proper husband and father I should be. His shoes will never fit my feet. I try them on from time to time. My father wasn't around to teach me. I don't think he knew himself.

My mother died before him. She tried to teach me everything possible to be a better person. Not knowing where to move or what to say, I stayed quiet. Standing up for the people you love was one thing she taught me. Though she rarely stood up for herself.

She also taught me not to hide behind a handicap. If you can't see the handicap, it doesn't make it any easier to hide behind it. We all have handicaps in which we hide behind. We won't admit to saying that either. Christ will light the way. The weight will be lifted and the pains dull.

When I get irritated, my heart sees the beauty in the world around me. When my mouth won't move, my heart sings praises to the Lord for those blessings I have – My wife, my daughter and my two sons (who are growing up without me).

You know, when I sit back and think about the times gone by... my father's shoes seem to get tighter by the year.

Iniquities of a father are passed down from one generation to the next. This I've come to understand. In understanding, I have to say that I cannot blame my father for the man that I am. I don't think he knew how to be the man he could have been. He had no guidance. I cannot blame my mother either. She did her best. I forgive them both. May they rest in peace!

My dear, you are a gift from God and that, I've known since the first day I saw you. If not you, there would be no other. No other person knows what I think or need, without my saying a word. My heart speaks to yours when we are apart. Your eyes sparkle and my heart dances at the sound of your laughter.

I will not hold on so tightly to the people who belong to Him in the first place. You and I will grow old together. Conquering each other's addictions and building up weaknesses that try to tear us down, I promise.

Our daughter will know, understand and walk in the ways of the Father. Joshua and William will be restored to me in His timing. As I shall become closer to my Father in heaven, becoming one with Him as I have with the one I love.

There is no greater gift than that of love. The love of the Father is very strong and undeniable. With each beat of a heart that so loved the world, we are placed in a time-released capsule. In time, all that we dream, want or need, will be given to us...for it is written, "Seek first the kingdom of God and all else shall be given unto you."

LIFTED ABOVE THE CLAY

Chapter Twenty-Eight

> "You are my servant, I have chosen you and have not cast you
> away: Fear not for I am with you; be not dismayed, for I am
> your God. I will strengthen you. Yes I will help you. I will
> uphold you with My righteous right hand."
> (Isaiah 42:9-10 NKJV)

In weakness, He becomes our strength. When darkness
nips at our heels, light is up ahead. When we are swallowed up
by angry voices telling us that we are not worthy of anything
better than our stuck lot in life, there is yet a clearer voice. One
that rebukes all the negative thoughts and statements we allow to
enter into our thinking. If we are still and pray, one voice can
give us the strength to bust loose. 'The Truth shall set us free.'

Demons flee when they hear the spoken word. Life and
death are in the power of our tongues. We need to be careful of
the words we use, for even in jest, the tongues are fast and will

141

lash out. Fear not, nor shall you lose hope or be anxious for anything. For when the time is right, our increase will come.

When that door is opened, no man can shut it for we will have favor with God and man in that season. Trust in the Lord as in no other and you shall see a change.

The treadmill has stopped and His mighty hand has caught you. All He needs from us is that first baby step. Since we must first drink of the milk as a child before we can eat of the meat of the Word, whatever we drink of His goodness and teachings will only fill us up until the hunger grows so strong that we cannot exist on milk alone.

The Lord is not a Lord of hatred but of love, yet He will let us back ourselves into a corner just so He can lift us from the clay in which we have gotten stuck.

FIRST MEETING...FIRE IN THE HEART OF A STRANGER
Chapter Twenty-Nine

'Seek first the Kingdom of God and the rest shall be given unto you.' The Lord promises us. He knew us before we were even here. In our hearts He places desires that He wants to see come to reality. Can we as humans find that desire and gift and realize that it's our calling to do what sets the Lord's heart afire with joy and happiness?

There are times when we give way to the world and give in to the flesh and do what we know would hurt our Father in heaven. As we do wrong, can we feel the tears as the Father cries over us. Yes, He allows us to be tempted and tested to see if we will lean on His will or our own.

I recently met a young man who doesn't waste time. He lives his life showing love to those we may not give a first glance at. I had heard that he spent Thanksgiving 2000 sharing turkey sandwiches with the homeless. Yes, he missed his family here in Washington but he wasn't going to let loneliness take over. He was in Colorado helping others. I don't know for sure if this man shared the Love of Christ with the people he ate with, but in that moment, Christ used this young man, thus Revelation 3:20 came to life.

'Behold, I stand at the door and knock. If anyone hears My voice and opens the door, I will come in to him and dine with him and he with Me.'

I was blessed in meeting Jason Schlegel when he was visiting home on his way to Japan. Our meeting was quick as I was at work. In that short time, I saw a lot of the Lord in him. I saw his mother's flare for life and the fire of the Lord in his heart.

Jason made a lasting impression on me. I won't soon forget it. I want to see Jason again and hope that we meet again. I want to hear his stories and see what the Lord has done in his life. I wish Jason well on his trip.

Do you remember the first time you met Christ? Will you recall the first time He said hello to you? He watches everything we do. He cries when we do wrong and rejoices when we do right. If we get into a rush, we may miss out on the gifts God has for us. The day I met Jason, I was in a rush. If his mother hadn't put up her hand and said, "STOP!" I would have breezed past my chance to meet her remarkable son, thus, losing out on one of God's greatest gifts...Jason!

Don't turn away from a person...you may just see the love of God wanting to talk to you. Take a moment and focus on the task. Live life to the fullest and make your life count.

LOOK BEYOND THE WHEELCHAIR

Chapter Thirty

How do you feed the hungry or shelter the homeless when you are the hungry and the homeless? This question comes to mind most often.

This morning I woke thinking, '*My dreams are so far off and I'm too tired to chase after them. I work, sleep, work and sleep...* '

I see myself one day not punching a time clock and taking life in strides. Enjoying life to the fullest as I make a living as a writer. There are places I want to go and things I want to do in my life, but I don't have the means to do it. That really stinks.

Writing about what you know is good, but when what you know is limited, then writing becomes repetitive. The same routine in life becomes the same stories on paper. Then I think of Jason Schlegel, a young man who always makes the most out of everything.

Now, isn't that just like the Lord to bring a thought, person or memory to mind to make us see that we have it good even in the midst of struggle?

When Jason was in school, he went to a dance set up at the local retirement home. Once there, he saw an elderly lady in a wheelchair. This positive young man went up to the lady and asked her to dance.

"No, thank you." She replied. "I cannot. I'm in this wheelchair."

"Nonsense." Jason said as he wheeled the lady onto the floor. He pushed her around and danced with her until she smiled from ear to ear. This young man helped this woman to feel like a million bucks. She was again young and alive.

Jason is a prime example of how you can make any situation work and have fun doing it. Life is only the pits if we eat all the fruits.

So, choose your words wisely and watch your steps. When you've fallen down and looking up, a hand will help you stand. Be thankful for what you have and don't stress, you will be blessed.

Jason showed me that you could be busy and still make every moment count...just look beyond the wheelchair and you can dance. I thank God for the moments of realization and I thank Jason Schlegel for being a person of love, kindness and action.

STOP THE TREADMILL

Chapter Thirty-One

Picture this... you're going through life, walking a treadmill, dealing with all the trials and joys. You've got your hands on the railing and turning up the speed one notch at a time. Before long, you're running in place... not going anywhere.

The storms of life are coming at you. You've either got all the time in the world or none at all. You've either got it all figured out or sitting in a fog. You're either in financial straights or freedom, carefree or knee-deep in troubles.

Your grip on the rails of the treadmill of life is getting tighter because you fear that if you let go, no one is there to catch you when you are propelled backwards by all the pressures of life's situations.

Humans make mistakes and then freak out about the choices we make in our daily lives. We feel we can never really trust anybody with the thoughts and things that bind us to the station in life where we are.

You reach top speed on the treadmill trying to break from the stress, but begin to wonder if even God will love you despite your faults. God doesn't blame you for being human because He made you that way.

Let go of the railing and let God catch you when you stumble. He will hold you up and lead you through life. Wrong things may happen due to the decisions made.

CLARITY COMES WITH TIME

With clarity there's understanding and a door will be opened. Trust and peace will eventually be the end result.

In the center of life's darkness a light will beam. Rejoice in the peace the Lord can bring and your eyes will see. The blinders will be dropped and the straps broken. No, problems will not just vanish but situations will be seen differently. Joy will fill your heart even in the midst of pain.

As Christians, people still have to walk through the trials and sometimes feel the emotions as non-Christians, but the insight is different. Doo-doo doesn't just happen. God can turn the bad into good...if you trust in Him.

Turn off the treadmill and walk at a slower pace. Take Christ by the hand and let Him lead you and your family in peace.

THREE STRANDS

Chapter Thirty-Two

In that single moment, just as the sunrise turns to daybreak, or a warm tear hits the floor, a heart feels a flutter of emotions. When the Harvest moon brings light to a darkened sky with its moonbeams through the trees, one can only know a true and honest love.

There is a love that comes from the Father in heaven and yet a blessing comes with it. That being, that there is a soul mate for everyone. Someone who knows your every thought yet doesn't question you for having given a wrong answer when a question is asked. Someone who never has to worry about trusting you because the love forged between two people is so strong that even distance can break that one true love.

Thank You Father God for the wife I have been given. She loves me for the one that I am and leaves my heart to itself, knowing that it only belongs to her. She listens to my words when I talk of the past. She knows that I speak not of what has been in order to dredge up the past but to learn for the lessons taught then. Not that the past was wrong, but that we all have to go through them in order to get to the current time in life.

Many people know of my pain and hurts but only my wife understands and hears what my heart truly says. It beats a tune she knows without doubt and her heart in turn returns the same beats. She and I are one even when we aren't together and even if we sound unsure at times, underneath, there is a sureness that is in all honesty and truth. I love her and she loves me. The two of us love the Lord. Three strands of love cannot be broken, burned or torn. Three hearts that create a circle that never ends, a never-ending love fest between my Father in heaven, my wife and I. Thus, without the two of them, I would surely die.

Thanks again Lord, for my loving, caring and trusting wife, Donna.

PEACE IN THE LION'S DEN

Chapter Thirty-Three

In the midst of the gray and the overcast of life, there has to be a garden. Love, song, great joy and deliverance, dancing, praise, worship, and tears of accomplishment aren't lost. Everything in life, whether it is the first step or the first stumble, blends into what the world calls life, that which we live day by day. But, do we ever notice the hours or the minutes we take for granted? Time is all we have and that in its self is a gift. A gift not to be placed on a shelf to gather dust, but rather a gift we are to incorporate into our movements of our very existence. This everyday love waits for us to stop and smell the roses. For some of us there may not be roses in the garden, whatever the flower or aroma that our life is filled with, there is a memory attached to it. Can we associate the smells of life with the good days and not just the bad moments we may have during our lifetime?

Look beyond the spider webs and see the freedom that our souls call for. There are times when my tongue lashes out the words I wish I'd never said to someone. At that very moment, my heart is reaching out with thoughts of love. As I desperately want to suck back in all the words that hurt, my heart's arms want to soothe the pain let loose. No, I cannot expect to be forgiven for the harm I unwontedly placed on another, but if I don't ask for forgiveness, I cannot expect that Jesus will forgive me either.

Laugh and smile when facing adversity thus feeling the weight of the world lifting. If I cannot climb out of this pit of lions I find myself in, then I shall praise the Lord even as the hungry killers eat me. As hunger can kill a human, it can also bring peace and life if we choose to see it in a new light.

In my most recent past, I was placed on the steps of death's door. Thought I wasn't all too sure if I was going to die or not, I was and am ready. I may have to kick the heck out of pride and use a cane to walk or slow down. That will come in time, I'm very sure of that.

I received in the mail a note that read: "Keep on writing". With that note was a check for $150. WOW!!! A true blessing that was. God knows His timing. I am encouraged by the reactions I get from my stories. I believe that I will make a living some day, but in getting that gift today I understand one thing. I am being paid for the gift God gave me. The payment may not always be financial but in words. The e-mails and letters I get, and the uses of my stories in other medias are a form of payment. I am deeply encouraged that I will see my four poetry books printed for the world to read even if it takes me a lifetime to save the $8,000 to print them all. Yet at this stage in the game, working to feed the family is more important than the manuscripts that sit on my desk.

The pain I feel daily is nothing compared to the ache my heart feels for those who do not know the love of Jesus. My heart cries out for them to seek the salvation that He offers. Those who know Him but have walked away make me sob as I pray. It is much harder to show the love of Christ to one who has turned away than it is to show it to one who is new and hungry for the gift He hands out.

I have prayed daily for a young lady at work who spent her eighteenth birthday in her car. She spent the holidays there as well. Yet she came to work and didn't say a word. She eventually moved in with a relative but that stay only lasted a few months. She extended her love to an animal and took it home with her. She told me that her pet had vanished from the home and she didn't know where it was. This young lady visited a local shelter and prayed that God would direct her to her dog. The dog was there, but upon coming home with the dog, this new

Christian was asked to leave. I had spoken to her about the love of Christ and the things He'd done for me in the past. She listened, but I had to let God work His magic. I saw this young lady reading her new Bible like she was a sponge. Thanks to her friend Sam, who got her to visit his church, God was able to answer my prayers. I talked with her about the Prayer of Salvation and wrote it down for her and asked her to say that prayer when she felt ready. She cried as she agreed. "Being a Christian isn't easy. Tests will be tossed at you to see if you will pass them or give in to the world and stop trying." I was told today that an apartment became available for her and her pet dog.

Now that is encouraging for me! It proves to me that we all have our "Den of Lions" we have to cope with, but even in the midst of hungry beasts, we can reach out with love and see God's hand reach down to lift us from the path of death.

In the words of Morrie from 'Tuesday's with Morrie', "Love one another or die." (If you've never read that book by Mitch Alborn or seen the just released movie, please do so.) Put your life in a clearer view. Spend Tuesday's with Morrie and your life with Christ. There just may be a lesson to be learned.

This story is for everyone. And to everyone I say "Thanks for the love, prayers and encouragement. A special thanks to Morrie and Mitch Alborn".

LOVE OF A FATHER

Chapter Thirty-Four

On the mountaintop I stand: Yelling, venting, letting my feelings out and not bottling them up. Who wants to hear it? I'm alone on this majestic spot, listening to my own voice echoing off the vast canyon. Will the answers vibrate back? I use this time to reflect on myself and who I really am.

"What would I do if God Himself were to show up and cop a squat next to me? Do I know enough to teach anyone? Would they care or even want to listen? Who knows? Holy Ghost, come stand by me. Help me to speak to my Father when I forget how to pray."

Closing my eyes, I see the everlasting glory of the Lord standing before me. His arms extended and palms out, beckoning me to know His love for what it is. He wants me to trust Him more than I am.

"I will not leave you, My child. I'm here with hands extended." His voice calm and gentle.

"Can I, Father, be worthy of Your love?" I ask.

"Oh, My child, all come short of the glory of God, yet I love you still. I shall love you always. My eyes are upon you and I cry when you cry and I rejoice with you in your time of triumph."

"But Lord..." my voice trailing off.

"I hear all that you pray for and I know all your needs. There is no need to worry. I will take care of you and those you love. Just trust Me."

I stood before my Lord speechless and in awe.

"Did I not send My angels to cover you in peace as you lay on your bed, face down in tears? Yes, My son, I watched as you and your wife cried in each other's arms. As your daughter comforted you with hugs. I too, held you in My arms. Everything will be fine."

"Father, place me in a place of authority and under authority. I ask for wisdom when I can no longer think. I understand that there may be lots for me to learn, but help me to pass that knowledge on. Help me to lead with caring and love and not a forceful hand. Give me a calm yet stern voice and not raving madness."

Though I may stumble and fall from time to time, I refuse

to let pain take over. Pain is pain but faith is stronger than that.

If He opens doors that no man can close and rolls out the pathway, would my faith be strong enough to step through the door? I hope so.

He wants to know if we trust Him enough to trust Him to guide our steps. All provisions have been made for our lives. He knows when the bad will strike. Though God isn't a bad God, He allows things to happen to us that we do not understand. This is to make us stronger in faith. We as humans do not know what's waiting for us at any given point, yet we must trust and press on. He knows the beginning and the ending of all things. He will not tempt us, but He will test us.

The question is... will we pass the test?

Chapter Thirty-Five

"I HEARD THE CRY OF AFRICA"

As the grave did not hold Jesus back
Nor shall life keep you
The vision you have seen
The cry you have heard
Your hunger for the people thrives
Spread the Gospel to the native tribes
A way has been prepared
Both before you and within you
If a man's gift makes room for him
Then so shall yours open the jungle
And the heart of Africa
You have heard their cries
As clearly as I've heard yours
Your passion for others
Will keep you going
Your love for your Lord
Will keep you safe
The jungle is dense
The road stony
But the gift you bring them

Comes from the heart of Me
Provisions have been made
Your prayer will be answered
As the grave did not hold Jesus back
Nor shall your fear keep you
For you have open hands
Thus opened My heart
You have trusted Me with your life

Now I will protect you
As you share the Gospel of My life
Be blessed and know that you are loved

In Matthew 11:10 it is written, 'Behold, I send My messenger before Your face, Who will prepare Your way before You.'

Miss Janet, as my daughter calls her, is full of fire, desire and compassion for God. She shows it in everything she does. From caring for her family, friends and the animals that share her life, to her unending and compelling yearn to know God more than ever before.

In the year and a half that I have known Janet, I've seen setbacks and moves forward. All of which were taken in stride. She finds laughter even in the darkest things. I've noticed that she has a heart for one thing, a vision given to her from God. She's heard the cry of Africa and strives to meet that challenge. Knowing that God wants her to be a missionary there, all things lead to that.

One Sunday a couple from Africa came to visit our church. Janet was wired from the get-go. Super glue couldn't hold her down. She ran around the church to the beat of FIRE IN THE HOUSE. She cried like a baby as she listened to John Michael and Evah as they talked of building orphanages and being the parents to some 200 orphaned children. When our visitors asked that our church continue to send missionary teams, Janet gladly mouthed, 'Take me, please, take me.' During the service I could see her leaving for Africa. Janet has been invited on a two-week missions trip to Kampala, Africa in December. This will be the true test.

I'm not sure how things will pan out for Janet, I do, however, understand one thing and I see it clearly. If a person has a vision given to them by God and it is matched by a desire of the heart, there is no returning to the old self. God opens doors and sets provisions for you to go through the door. No man can stop a vision of God's from reaching the person of His choice. The only wall would be that person's denying that the vision is there and not acting on it.

Janet thrives for the things of God and therefore her heart belongs to Him and she obeys the Word. He in turn answers prayers. I cannot see with the human eye how she will get to Kampala, Africa. Yet, I know that Janet not only dreams of Africa, but she has heard the cry of Africa. That voice will see her through and she will survive.

May the Lord keep her and give her a strategy to get the funds to reach her destination, both in December 2001 and beyond.

A CALL TO RISE

Chapter Thirty-Six

The enemy lingers on the border, waiting for a chance to pounce. A doorway to enter in and destroy what God has put together. Can we see the enemy when he starts his prowl? Can we stop him from advancing onto our camp and stealing what rightfully belongs to God?

Now is the time for all men to come to the aide of their wives and loved ones. As a man twice married and having seen the destruction left by the forces of the lord of darkness, I implore the men of God to rise up, hit their knees and pray like never before.

All things work out for those who love the Lord. The trick is to know which voice is heard and which move is right. How can we tell if an open door is opened by Jesus or by the enemy? Who benefits from our actions? Gratify the flesh and see the relationship die.

Be bold and strong, take your wife's hand and pray. There's nothing stronger in the spirit realm than a family who prays through the tough times. At some point we are all faced with the decision to walk out or brave the storms ahead. The enemy may entice with objects of beauty to get a man to fall, but while he is on the floor, he can win the fight with prayer. Resist the devil and he must flee.

Great is the gift of marriage and family. Strong is the foundation built with God as its cornerstone. Calm is the storms when He is the center of marriage.

I'm not perfect by any means. I've fallen several times. Backsliding farther than the time before, till I've hit rock bottom. Remembering though, that even as I've stepped away, Jesus is waiting for me to return. He gave us the choice to say 'Yes' or 'No'. He will not stop us from choosing this way or that, but He will lovingly wait for us to repent. Then He will forgive us, if we allow ourselves to let go of our 'self' and let Him guide us with His love.

If a wife strives to do the will of the Father, but her husband wants to do it his way, then eventually the enemy will explode and have his way. Thus, the same will happen if a man wishes to serve God and his wife doesn't. Don't be deceived, if a married man leaves his wife to 'get right with God', but spends his time playing the field and not 'searching for the Father' then he's fooling himself. God will not tempt man to make him fall. Marriage is a union warranted and sanctioned by God. By making God the center of our marriage, we can weather any storm the enemy sends our way.

"...having been built on the foundation of the apostles and prophets, Jesus Christ Himself being the chief cornerstone, in which the whole building being fitted together, grows into a holy temple of the Lord, in whom you also are being built together for a dwelling place for God in the Spirit."

As men of God, both single and married, we are called to be the spiritual leaders of our homes. Praying and reading the Word is our responsibility. If there is no man in the house then the woman must take that stand and fight to keep the structure of family together.

God inhabits the praises of His people and knowledge come from hearing the Word. So, if darkness peeks around the corners, sing and praise, run, jump and call out to God and the darkness will be swallowed by the Light and love of Jesus.

The iniquities of a father are passed down from generation to generation. Our children follow our example. If a man yells at his wife and then decides to take 'the easy way out' our sons may very well take that as okay. But if we as men spend quality time with our kids and read to them and pray with them, then the iniquities will stop and the seeds of love will be planted. "And you, fathers, do not provoke your children to wrath, but bring them up in the training and admonition of the Lord."

Don't freak out if it seems that your words fall on deaf ears. If anyone who has ears can hear the words of God then eventually the message will take. Only God knows a man's heart. If we ask God to beat us up until we can no longer run from Him, He will. But not in the sense of smacking us with a bat, but rather letting other men of God cross our paths with the same message we first chose to ignore. 'We may get tired of people telling us how to do this or that', but if we stop and listen, we may just see it as confirmation of what He wants us to do.

Life will not be easier if we place the shoe on the other foot or remind a person of their fault and pass mistakes. Turn away from the world and embrace the teaching of God and see how strong we become. If a man knows he has to be beaten and weak before going to his Father to see his way clear, then why doesn't he skip the beating and go right to the Father to start with? Forget playing 'ring around the mulberry bush' or 'catch me if you can'. No matter how much we think we know what's best for us, the Father always knows best. So make like an arrow and head straight for the target. This is a call to rise. Step up with bended knee and pray.

LIVE IN PRAYER

Chapter Thirty-Seven

"The prayer of a righteous man is powerful and effective."

This statement comes to mind more and more these days as I watch marriages of people I care for fall apart at the seams. Where are we going wrong as men in these families? I know that prayer can hold a family together, but wouldn't we have a stronger chance if we were on the same track? The goal is to make God happy and do right by Him. Who do you think suffers from within the enemy's wake of a split? The children? God? How about everyone?

My first marriage, though I knew would end even before it started, produced two blessings. In 1991, Joshua David was born. In 1992, William Charles was born. I tried to make the marriage work despite our ages and controlling in-laws, but I was fighting a one sided battle.

I often went to God in prayer, but "we" as a couple never did that. I made my wife my world and in doing that I got ran over by the enemy. I believed in God but wasn't strong enough to stand up for what I believed in. Giving in to everything that my wife wanted invited the enemy into our lives and there he set up home. I was far from righteous. I wasn't sure if my prayers for a Godly wife and marriage were reaching God. I stood on the fence, wanting my cake and eating it too.

In 1994, my marriage ended. Why couldn't I make it work? Why didn't I stick it out? Man cannot make anything work by his own strength, but in God and with God, all things are possible.

As a single man, I sought God with everything I could, but the enemy was still getting to me. How? Through my desires to see my children when I knew I'd never see them again. Death seemed to be the only way out. It was then that God reached in and removed me from the grasp of darkness and set me straight.

I hadn't seen Joshua since he was nineteen months old, nor have I seen William since he was three months old, yet now I know that one day, I will see them. I pray for them always. My new wife, Donna, who loves God more than she'd ever love me, also prays for them.

I kept in touch with my boys regularly until Joshua's fifth birthday, when his mother asked me to give him and his little brother up for adoption. I calmly said "No." She hung up the phone. Since then, I've had to leave them in God's hands.

Being related to men who have left their wives for reasons I cannot understand, I have to ask why they would not want to be around their children from their marriages. I have been told that "God wants these men to start over, fresh from lies and mistakes."

Understanding that statement is clear. To me that's a lie told to these men by the father of lies himself. Children are not a lie, nor are they mistakes. We are blessed with children for a reason. I, for one, wish I could have seen my boys grow up. But my not seeing them wasn't my choice. I hold no hard feelings for the decisions their mother has made in the aftermath of our breakup, but I pray that when the kids are ready, they want to see me and know me. If they choose not to let me in as their father, then maybe I can be their friend. I pray that they are walking with God.

I may not have the answers to the questions Joshua and William will one day have for me. I rest in knowing that when that time comes about, Jesus will give me the words.

Fathers, I ask you, no matter what type of situation you

are in, don't turn your back or your heart on the children you love. If your marriage is busting up for whatever reason and you cannot reach out to your wife or God, then reach out to the kids.

I pray that God will be able to touch the hearts of the men of this nation and turn their hearts back to their families.

Peace to the men as we LIVE IN PRAYER.

...AND THE SURVIVOR IS?
Chapter Thirty-Eight

Congratulations to the "ultimate survivor", Tina Wesson, for having come out on top of the game to win the million dollars. Hats off to Colby Donaldson for supporting Tina all the way in the true Texan style, and being the "runner up".

My heart leaped as I watched the telecast on the eve of the 42nd day in the Australian outback, when Tina and Colby both said that the game was over. The winner of the game had not been announced and yet they both won the game.

They found joy in reaching the end. Yes, they played the game with mental and physical strength, but the one thing that pulled them through was the compassion of their hearts. God was there even if they didn't realize it at the time.

Mike falling into the fire wasn't a pleasant site to see but a realization. To know that directions may change in a second.

The flames of a fire may have ended Mike's trek in the outback, but he became a vessel to be used by God. Like he said, "Not even a million dollars could pay for that experience."

Seeing Tina swim across the raging river to rescue the canister of rice showed me that God had His hand on her. He protected her. When she stood on that pole out in that water for as long as she did, only to give her shot at immunity to Keith, showed that God had her heart.

Colby's day of triumph began when he voted Keith off over Tina, thus clinching her victory, and reached a high point when he picked Tina up in his arms when they revealed her as the winner.

As I watched strangers' lives change thousands of miles away, I too, was blessed. Blessed in knowing that I don't have to leave home to find what I was given.

Living with Cerebral Palsy, every day is a reward challenge and every night is a tribal council. In the past few years walking has become more difficult. My reward is being able to walk from one end of the house to the other without falling. I count myself lucky if I fall down once, but I'm tired if I fall about the fifth time. I began to ask "Why" even though I know the answer.

Every night I sit at "tribal council" and wait to see if satan will try to vote me out of my life as I try to find immunity with Jesus Christ. (The power of prayer is wonderful.)

No, I didn't apply for a game that I know would do me in within the first three days. No, I didn't win a million dollars for having lasted forty-two days in a strange land. This world is a strange land in which we were placed to live out the lives we were given. Some friends I know have gone home to be with Jesus while the rest of us struggle to adapt to life here on earth.

I have survived thirty-two years here on this planet and have learned many lessons I hope to pass on to my children. Anyone who was once lost or caught up in the darkness, but can find even the slightest reason to strive for the next day...they are the survivors!

WHEN WE RUN
Chapter Thirty-Nine

"If you extend yourself to help the hungry and satisfy the afflicted soul, then your light shall dawn in the darkness, and your darkness shall be as noon day." ISAIAH 58:10

In this rat race and daily grind, we've come to know as our existence, we tend to set our sights on a goal with the intention of going after it. We enter a "tunnel vision" as we aim in the direction of the target. However, we miss it by a mile. Seldom do we hit the mark.

After countless stumbles, will we ever get it right? We fill our hearts with hopes. Reaching out for the last breath that could be smothered from us at any moment. Wanting and yearning for clarity and peace of mind. Hungering for more than this life has to offer, we pray and ask for time to get to know God.

He is happy and willing to show us who He is, but in doing that, He will show us ourselves. When the time comes for us to reflect, we run for anything that shows itself more appealing. How strange is that? Is it just a man thing, or just plain humanistic? It's fear.

We fear that if we take time to reflect on ourselves, we may be forced to look at our true self. We battle against one another. Or so it seems, when what's really going on is this...there are demons that cannot be seen by the human eyes, sitting on our shoulders.

These little puppets of the devil try to drive a wedge in where it doesn't belong. They succeed in their mission when we give in to what we know is wrong. Thus missing what are giving to us when it isn't there, but not knowing how to hold onto the blessing when it is there.

Stop running from the very One who can make everything better. The devil gets a kick out of watching us run like mad trying to figure out which way to go. Why is it that we give into the very thing that has satan laughing all the way to the grave. Beats me. Must be that humanistic thing again. Or is it that we haven't learned to slow down and listen. We often say things before we should or we take off on an "I can do this on my own" tangent instead of waiting or asking for help.

Yes, we could probably do anything and everything on

our own and that is good to some degree, but we have been placed on this planet to help each other in whichever way we can. If someone needs help and you can give it without asking "What's in it for me?" then you will truly be blessed in the end. But, if you're the type of person who's not going to help without seeing the "return" first, then think of the phrase, "What goes around comes around".

There are sacrifices that have to be made from time to time. It is in those times we show our true character. When we run to escape the sacrifice, we are just running from the blessing that is waiting on the other side.

Who's character do you want others to see? The one you see in the mirror or Christ's? The next time you see your reflection, think of who you really see.

HIS LIGHT THROUGH THE TRIALS

Chapter Forty

Dear Friends, family and readers. I have to be honest to you and myself. I live to write and reach the hearts of the nations.

"The poor is not he who is without a cent, but without a dream"- Daniel Broner

As I watch satan attacks many marriages around me. I failed to see that he was bombarding my own marriage. The more I preached to those around me, the less I saw what was happening here at home. How fast can things switch? In the blink of an eye, life can be turned upside down.

ANGEL KISSES:

She wakes with excitement, "The moon is asleep and the

sun is awake." Ready to battle the day with all the joy a four-year-old can.

Quietly as her daddy sleeps, she kisses his cheek and presses her warm face to his as if to hug him. Softly she says, "I love you, Daddy."

He lay there with tears forming in the corner of his closed eyes. A smile crosses his face as his little one runs off.

SATAN'S ATTACK:

A husband wakes up riddled with pain from the last night's work. Though his room was bright with the summer's sun and his wife lay quietly next to him, depression and darkened thoughts settled in his mind.

"I want to die. I'm tired of this way of life. I know what I want to do and the more I strive to get there, the further behind I fall. I need help." He screamed and yelled of his deepest hurts. As he drove off to work, he cried. At work he cried more and thought of suicide. On the way home he prayed, "God, please help us make this work. Help us to meet our debts and see this marriage survive and not scatter to the winds."

HIS PROMISE:

"For I was hungry and you gave Me food; I was thirsty and you gave Me drink; I was a stranger and you took me in."
MATTHEW 25:35

This man and this woman were two strangers brought together in the Lord's family. There He shed over them, His tears and bled from His heart, the love He wanted to show them. God foresees their lives from beginning to end. He watches as they goof up, backslide, back up and back out. He protects even when they are thought to be out in the cold. His promises are YES and AMEN.

These two people were brought together as one from very different places and though in the world it seems that they will not make it, God can and will hold them together, but first they have to break. Breaking together is better than breaking apart. God can fix anything but it is easier to fix what is already broken when it breaks first.

TRANSLATION:

I have said this many times to myself and to others. "I may write well, because it is a God given gift to bless others with, but I wish I could live the way that I write, thus enjoying what others see."

Renew my mind, Lord, and help me to love as You have loved me. You don't bring people together to see them kill one another, but rather to help lift each other up. Before I can be of any help to those around me, Father God, I ask that You start here in my heart and my home. Make us to be the couple You want to see shining on a mountain top and not hiding under cover.

You say that a man without a vision returns to his past. I have a vision and I want to take hold of it and live it out! You gave me that vision. I believe You want me to live it.

Enter into the hearts of every married couple who is feeling the onslaught of satan and his army, and turn them into the prayer warriors who will not give in, but fight the great fight of love. With you as their leader, they will refuse to hide behind excuses and become the husbands and wives You called them to be.

Help those who have drawn weary to gather strength to step up. Carry those who cannot lift their feet. Help to lift the weight of a lifetime of wrongs with the power of right choices. Tell them that they can do it. Alone they are but dust blowing in the wind, but together they can form a bond. And with You, Father, that bond will be a force to reckon with. AMEN! AMEN! AMEN!

LIKE A SNAKE
Chapter Forty-One

The words we speak release spirits within them. Life and death are in the power of the tongue. Speaking negative all the time towards someone will result in that person acting negatively. Positive words ignite positive actions.

Without realizing it, we also give our words wings. One person's words can either build up or bring down a whole room.

The other day I received an email from a friend. I was reminded that we couldn't serve both God and Mammon. That is so true. It isn't how much money we have, but where our hearts are aimed. Releasing our own control and letting God take over. We tend to be backseat drivers. We want God to drive us where He wants to take us, but we want to tell Him how to get us there.

Take off the blinders that keep us seeing what we think is the problem and look at the real reason. Stop the demon in its tracks. We are known for the fruits we bare. Let the fruits be positive. We should be as wise as a serpent:

1.   Snakes have no limbs. So they do what the head says. (God is the head of the church. We need to leave our hands to ourselves and try not to step on or over others as we get where we're going.).

2.   Snakes do not have ears. They cannot hear what's being said so they're not affected by discouraging words.

3.   Snakes have no eyelids. They don't sleep and are always aware of what's around them. They see their target and go for it. Letting nothing get in the way. (We want God. We should head for Him in a safe way.)

4.   Snakes are voiceless. They do not backbite or gossip. (Keep our tongues quiet.)

5.   Snakes grow all the time, leaving their old skins and taking on new skins. (Killing the old man and taking on the characteristics of Christ.)

6.   Snakes inhabit every nation. (Go throughout the world.)

7.   Snakes only have one lung. They cannot breath in two sources at the same time. (Take in what God wants for us and not the world...God or Mammon? God or money?)

It is good to have money to live, but to live to get money can kill a person or a marriage.

Give up control to God and let Him lead you through.

WHILE YOU LOVED ME
Chapter Forty-Two

It was a dark and still Texas morning the day she went home. Leaving wasn't her choice, but it was her time and she knew she had to go. She had no idea how her death would effect those she left behind, but God knew and He knew everything was going to be okay.

I was seventeen when that day arrived. On August 1st, 1986, my mother's battle with cancer ended while in a nursing home nearby. It wasn't easy to say good-bye to the woman who tried so hard to show her love for me by letting me live my life without motherly barriers. Her life wasn't perfect and yet there were lessons to be learned in her forty-eight years. "I will never forget those things you did while you loved me, Mom."

"ACTIONS SPEAK LOUDER THAN WORDS"

I didn't realize how much she cared nor did I stop to find out.
She was up before dawn each day off to work, and home before
dusk. The bills were paid and the meals were made,
 I thought those were things a mother did.

Days off were spent playing cards or having water fights.
Never did she say, "I love you", never did she say, "I care"
As the days passed, I knew those words because she was there.
Now she's been gone for fourteen years, her memory stuffed in
my mind, items that were hers stored in boxes.

I'm getting older, she cannot. I have children she's never known.
God gave a gift to me. As a baby she rocked my cradle. As a
teen she rocked my world. Love doesn't have to be spoken.
Actions speak louder than words.

The angels came to call in the early morning hours of
May 6th, 2001. For a long while Earl Campbell lived with the
pains of getting old and knew that one-day his trip home would
begin. On that day, at the age of seventy-eight, this gentle man
of God looked up to heaven and smiled. I don't know for sure if
he ever knew how he affected those around him, but as his
neighbor and friend, I can tell you he was deeply loved and
greatly respected. He may have been up there in age, but that of
the youngest person could not match even his spirit. We talked
many times and compared the trials of aches and pains with
laughter. We prayed healing over each other. "Earl, you beat me
there. God healed you before me. But I'll catch up to you yet,

my friend. Life isn't the same here without you, but I will remember the strength you showed while you loved me."

"YOU'RE A MAN OF GOD"

Your steps are slow but steady
Your voice deep yet loving
Your hands firm yet gentle
Your touch melts a heart of stone
Your eyes soothe an angry soul
Your laughter places a child at ease
Your heart speaks truth to what it sees
You make a family member out of a stranger
You calm a fearful spirit
Your concern makes you strong
Though your body may be weak
Your cheeks warmed with love
Your questions don't condemn
You listen before speaking
You speak without words
You may stumble from time to time
You shall never fall
For My hand comes down from heaven
In the moment of your call
Compassion bursts within you
Clearly this is seen
Love isn't fearful
Yet open and free
Keep giving love to the people
For in you they see Me

2000 years ago a man walked these roads. He was born with the intention of dying. He became a teacher even as he was taught. He showed love and compassion everywhere he went. His story has been written and his love lives on.

On the day of his death the angels sang. The earth rattled and the skies rolled back. He looked into the eyes of those who loved him and knew he had done what he was born to do. He gave life to many he knew and a world he didn't. I don't know if I could have handled watching him die that way. "I do know that I get strength and joy from knowing that He died to show that a parent will go to any length to protect... while they love you."

"TRAVEL'S END"

He knew His path what He must do
To take our sins from me and you
He spoke of wisdom more than we knew
His love for His Father was stronger than glue
To take the steps in which He did
Gave way to death for One
But life for many upon the cross He went
He felt the nails He saw the blood
His travels came to an end
On Calvary

The air was still
As the skies listened
The earth began to tremble
The heavens rolled
His last breath taken
Light shown on darkness

TESTIFY TO LOVE

Chapter Forty-Three

From his birth the eyes of God the Father watched him. He was cared for by his earthly mother and taught by his earthly father. The hearts of the world called out for him. As he grew older he was lead by the voice of God and God's hand was upon him.

Are we worthy enough to have the very voice of God whispering to our hearts? Do we deserve to have the coverage of His Mighty hand? By human standards we do not deserve His love and protection, but rather to die by the consequences of our actions. "The wages of sin is death."

God watched as Jesus walked this earth speaking of love and kindness to all. No matter what a person's station was in life, He reached out to save a life.

Many listened and promised to keep His word, yet there

were others who hated Him for who He was and feared what He stood for. Even in their hatred, He loved.

Forced to leave the cities and towns, he taught from the mountaintops and valleys. Some followed and others did not. In time, everyone would hear and know the truth.

On the day of His death, He took all the sins of the entire world upon Himself. Thus becoming our sins. His Father in heaven had to turn His eyes from His only Son. We should love the person but no the sin.

Daily we are put through a test. Can we pass that test? Each step we take is one step closer to victory. With every kind word spoken, we get the upper hand. When we think we have it bad, there is always someone who has it worse. What we have is never enough. Wanting more or wanting to be better is what seems to drive us.

There is a war that is going on that some can see and others don't; yet every heart can feel it. Are we strong enough to fight on the front lines? Are we ready to say 'yes' when asked to move up in battle, or are we still on the fence?

At the time of our birth, we had nothing but life and love. In other words, we had it all. As we grew up we were conditioned to want what we didn't need and overlook what we did need.

The true reason for life is to love and to share truth in

love. But we strive for material things. Anything that money can buy, we want. There's nothing wrong with having money. Money cannot make a person happy. It's what you do with the money that pleases the heart.

When Christ died, we were given back everything we once had at birth. Jesus gave us it all. Are we ready to testify to that kind of love and give our all so someone else's heart can have a new life?

If Christ were to ask, "did you love others with all your heart? Did you do everything you could to see that someone was happy?"

Can you say, "Yes, I can testify to that."

HIS ONLY TEAR

Chapter Forty-Four

"Whoever finds his life will lose it, and whoever loses his life for My sake will find it." (Matthew 10:39)

Why is it always darkest before dawn?
Before the sun set
And dark shadows appear
His heart cried out
For his child to hear
The demons arrived
Blackness fell hard
Away went his child
With his child went his heart
In the distance
The hours passed
Teardrops fell
In a painful
Bloody crash
Years go as the day breaks
Evil murkiness stays
He smiles with laughter
His heart aches

No child to raise
No "Daddy" phrase
No first step taken
Nor first word spoken
Just a clip-on bow tie
As a small token
Will dawn ever come?

(February 26, 1992)

Tears swelled in his eyes as the new daddy held the tiny body in his arms. His legs trembled and his body shook at the thought of living without his child.

How will I ever explain this to you? Will you understand? I pray that you'll forgive me, but at this point in life, little man, I think I'd understand if you grew up hating me as I did your grandfather.

He held his eight month old closely to his chest. Savoring and recording into memory, every sound and movement Joshua David made. His tiny heart beating largely against his tiny chest.

Too hard! It is too hard to cram a lifetime of father and son happiness into a few hours. Eight months was just too short. I want to watch you grow, laugh and cry. I want to be there for you and love you, the way a father should be there for his son. On June 22, 1991, when Joshua David was born, all his father thought of was being the best dad a boy could ever want despite

192

the limitations. But now, due to irreconcilable differences, those thoughts would remain in a dream.

God is the only one who can help. This sad daddy thought as he stared at the bundle of joy asleep in his arms... for the last time. Those small fingers wrapped around a forefinger, all those delicate muscles and tendons in one small body. Those fingernails. A father's eyes moved to J.D.'s feet, tracing his toes with a gentle hand.

I cannot believe God blessed us with this little miracle. I thank God every day for the gift of your life.

A father's hand moved from J.D.'s tiny feet to his hands, then his head, running his hand over the baldness. Tracing the blonde eyebrows and lashes. His son, their son, was perfect.

The baby stretches as his tiny hands reached for the air and his mouth opening wide welcoming oxygen to the brain. The bluish-gray windows to his soul looked up at his daddy with hope and innocence.

Again, his father wondered if his son would ever understand, or if he would grow up hating his father.

Time was precious and short. Would it be possible to freeze this moment in time? There was happiness in holding his son. That happiness was shattered...

It has been nearly ten years since Joshua David was born and nearly as long since I've seen him or his younger brother,

William. Every year, as their birthdays get close, I wonder if I'll ever see them again. Will my prayers be answered? Will they even know who I am? Do they know of me? Will they want to know me? Will they even listen to me if given the chance? Do they know where to find me or want to find me?

I use to send letters all the time to their last known address but they all came back. I've kept those letters, but returned letters cannot fill the void.

Now I know how God must feel. God watches His children throughout their lives. He talks to those who will listen and He prays for those who stray. He wants us to talk with Him and get to know Him, but we must choose if we want to. If things go wrong in our lives we blame Him for allowing it to happen. If things are going great we take the credit ourselves. I chose to leave a marriage that wasn't healthy, but losing contact wasn't my choice.

God doesn't want to lose contact with us, but he waits to see if we want to be a part of His life. In time, though life may seem to repeat its self, it will come full circle and all will turn out for the best. Rest assured, we may go through life like mice in a maze, but the end is the end and God knows just that.

As in the years past, another poem will be written this June 22nd, the only gift I know to give. It will be placed in a book and saved for the day we finally meet. HAPPY 10th

BIRTHDAY, Joshua David. I loved you on the day of your birth and I'll love you always. Love, the father you probably don't remember. God remembers us, and our lives are in His hands.

"Do not be afraid; do not be discourage." (Joshua 8:1)

TO THE FATHER
Chapter Forty-Five

For years she'd done this. It was nothing out of the ordinary for her. Every year the young lady returned to this spot. Flowers cradled in the crook of her arm as she walked the same path her father went down. She felt closer to him on this day for some reason. Her heart knew she was close to him. Stopping just before her destination, looking here and there. Familiar to the surroundings, she knelt down.

"Happy father's day, Dad." She replaced the wilted flower in the vase with fresh cut daisies. "I know you are at peace now that you are in Heaven, but my heart still aches over you being gone. But, one day, we will be together again."

In a rush to get to work, the young man glances into his daughter's room and find her asleep. How peaceful she looks. He gently kisses her face then runs out the door. Hours flash by in a combustible burst of energy. Worn by the day, he drives home.

The sun begins to set beyond the pasture. The horses graze on the grass, their bodies glistening in the remaining light of the sun's rays. What a sight. Nature at its finest. The young man opens the car door and exits the vehicle in pain. Slowly he walks to the ramp and reaches for the railing. Stopping only once to glance at the setting sun. A tug on his shirt catches his attention. He looks down. There, before him, stands his little girl. Her brown hair flowing in the gentle breeze and her brown eyes dance with excitement. Her face radiant with energy and love as she tosses her arms around his waist. "Oh, Dad, I'm glad you're home. I missed you all day. Happy Father's Day Dad."

He squats down and they embrace. Lost in a moment that only a father and his child can share.

She was there when they nailed Him to the cross. She listened to His final words. The blood dripped from His body. The thorns on His head looked painful. Those nails, how intense were they? This man didn't harm anyone, but this is what He gets. Nailed to a cross between two thieves. Only the skies and the earth stated how they felt. People ran for cover and others bowed their heads, knowing He was an innocent man.

For three days she prayed. She wondered to herself and asked, "Why?" Though she was tired, she watched to see if the guards would take the body of her dead Master. But no, they fell asleep. She too, wanted to close her eyes and drift off, but dared not to. In the glare of a bright moon, the stone rolled away. In the entryway an angel stood.

"Behold, He has risen." She heard him say.

She smiled at the thought. *The gift our Father gave us, is now given back to the Father.*

A father never leaves his children alone even when his children want to go it alone. The heart of the Father knows the hearts of the fathers. If in our hearts, we desire to please the Father, we shall see it come to life...even in the hour of our death.

So, to all the fathers on earth, I send you blessings on this day, which is to be yours. Live well and to the fullest. In time, you shall receive rest.

ANGELS HAVE A HOME

Chapter Forty-Six

Where the human eye fears to look, may be the home of angels. We are not sure where they are or when they will appear. We fear the unfamiliar and uncomfortable. And why shouldn't we? We've all been wronged at one point or another, so we've placed up a shield.

We make decisions to make our lives easier. Those decisions may turn out to be a mulberry bush for God to go around. No matter how He does it, His plan will be fulfilled in our lives.

When a green pasture turns to silver clouds beneath a full moon, in there lies a glimpse of a realm beyond this earth. It is a place of peace and comfort for those who no longer reside here, but grace the heavens and dance to the tunes in our hearts.

The Lord wept for the mothers and fathers whose

children went from the womb to the arms of God without having sounding their first cry.

He sings out for the little ones who are born prematurely and fight for the life they breathe for. He sees that they grow strong even as they stay fragile, to inspire others.

He looks for compassion in the hearts of those who have no desire to have children, and then places a drug-addicted baby in their arms, knowing that an angel has found a home.

Having lost two kids through divorce and two through miscarriages, I understand the pain and hurt. There are times when I still wonder "why?" I still shed tears and want to blame myself for the loss, yet the love for them and the many children of this world, grows ever so strong.

I am but one man whom may not be able to do much for anyone out there, but if there is one person out there; man, woman, teen or child, that I may reach out to, so be it to be my mission in life.

God loves us all and though He allows us to walk through life with pains and hurts, He doesn't let us do it alone.

On earth we learn to walk, run and ride a bike. In doing that, we skin our knees, get up and move on. They are life lessons we've remembered and overcome, but do we ever stop during our daily trials and think of what's going on above us?

Why do we have to beat around the mulberry bush to

have what our heart's desire? Why do we want Him to have to do the same? All He wants is to give us our hearts desire.

In the light of a full moon, I saw angels on their knees. Some weeping, some praising, some praying, some dancing for joy, but all were watching. Some of them I knew and some I didn't. I couldn't hear them on that clear July night, but I seen they were all right with where they were.

After seeing that I no longer wanted to blame myself for the losses I had felt, nor did I wonder "why?" I just knew peace. I'm not saying that I won't ever ask the "Why" question again in my life, because I am only a man. I don't understand the reasons behind people dying "before their appointed time", or why someone dies before doing what he or she was placed on this earth to do. Please, don't take this wrong or think of me as being harsh. Yes, there are many questions that pop up, and to a lot of them I have yet to find answers.

On a cool clear July night, clarity came about: Both here on earth, or above the clouds, there are angels, and they are watching over us. Either in our hearts or in our arms, angels have a home.

WITNESS IN THE SILENCE: ANGELS WATCH OVER US

Chapter Forty-Seven

Sometimes life changing impressions are made not by spoken sounds, but the voice of silence when words are not enough.

A young wife, alone at night as her husband works, prays *God, protect me and keep me safe. Please place angels around this home and around me, so I will not fear the night.*

There at the foot of her bed he sat, a tall and quiet man. Silent in voice, yet his brown eyes spoke volumes of confidence and strength. His hair slightly long but not shoulder length. His hands laced over a bended knee. His clothing was white. He wore open toed sandals with straps laced up to the knee. He said nothing as his charge studies him. One of his hands equaled both of hers. His face was tan and peaceful. Off his shoulder, the young lady saw a set of wings folded into his back. He sat there, saying nothing and going nowhere.

This young wife feared nothing as she wondered which angel paid her this visit. She turned over and drifted off to sleep.

When she woke, the gentle giant (who could have stood nine feet tall had he gotten up) was gone.

* * * * *

Within the womb a child is cradled. Surrounded by fluids and the essence of life. From the outside no one can see, beneath the child there is a hand. Not the child's hand, one Mightier than she. She sleeps, unaware of the life that waits for her birth, in the palm of the hand of Jesus.

Face down on the floor a woman cries from pain and heartache. Eighteen months ago a drug-addicted baby was placed in her arms. Though she didn't want another child of her own, in her heart of hearts this child had become hers. After loving and caring for little Laura through the withdrawals from the drugs that had been part of her body since before she was born, Laura was returned to her birth mother.

"I can not do this. Nor do I understand why You would allow a child so small and sweet to become a part of this family if she was going to be taken. Show me why. I lift it up to You because this is too big for me to deal with."

As the woman prayed she saw a baby cradled in the hand

of Jesus, then heard, "I was in control then and I'm in control now. This isn't just the child you cared for, but it is you. I have you in my hand. Trust Me now, with your life as I have trusted you with Laura's. Yes, you will feel pain and you will cry, but you shall know the comfort of peace."

* * * * *

A young girl looks into the bare cupboards and sees nothing but canned food as she cries, "I want some cereal."

Her father prays as his wife prepares peanut butter toast. "It isn't cereal, but thank God for the simple meal, amen."

"Amen," their daughter says with a smile.

That night, two boxes of cereal were given to the girl's father.

"Daddy, cereal. YUM!" She hugged her daddy, ate cereal, and then went to bed with a full tummy.

"Sleep well, Sweetie." Her daddy whispered as a tear ran down his cheek.

A few days later a phone call came.

"Be at the gas station near your work at 10:30am tomorrow."

"May I ask what this is about?"

"Just be there."

The man looked at his wife, "I'm not sure what this is,

but I'll wait here while you go pay what bills you can. Hopefully we'll know what's going on by the time you get back."

Minutes passed with a strange silence. If Trish knew what was going on, she wasn't saying anything.

Suddenly, Arlene, the fuel center supervisor appeared across the parking lot. "Come here." She waved. "Someone came by this morning and left this for you. This person said that you needed these things."

"What?" Felix asked.

Just then Dottie, a friend and co-worker drove up. Arlene opened her trunk to reveal groceries galore. "This is a gift from someone who cares and when your wife comes back, take them home."

"Who was it?" Felix asked.

"I can not say." Arlene and Dottie smiled.

The next night as Felix was getting off work, a young co-worker says, "Don't close down yet." Then walks off to the soap aisle only to return with a large bottle of bleach. "Ring this up for me."

"Sure. You going to clean tonight?"

"No. It isn't for me." The kid said. He took the bleach and headed for the exit along with a customer.

As Felix went to get into his car, he noticed the bottle of

bleach on the floorboard of the front of his car.

Three nights later, as Felix was leaving work, again he thanked God for the gift of food. Stuffed in the car door was a note written on an envelope: IT'S WHAT I HAD LEFT. HOPE IT HELPS. I KNOW IT'S NOT MUCH.---J

In his car, Felix sat and prayed, *Father God, what is this and who has left it?* After a moment of silence, Felix opened the envelope to find folded in it, ten dollars. He pressed the cash to his lips and simply prayed, *My Father in heaven, Thank You for the angels who watch over me. Bless those who gave all that they had, just so I could have enough. Watch over those whose actions act as witnesses in the silence when words are not enough.*

THE JABEZ PRAYER

And Jabez called on the God of Israel saying,
"Oh, that you would bless me indeed,
and enlarge my territory,
that Your hand would be with me,
and that You would keep me from evil,
that I may not cause pain!"
So, God granted him what he requested.
(1 Chronicles 4:10 NKJV)

Standing in the field of life, pondering the past, looking at the 'now' and leaving tomorrow where it is. Life isn't one that should be controlled by humans. Let God get in the driver's seat.

What a concept. Tossing up your arms, palms flat and skyward, saying, "Use me." Then saying the Jabez prayer. Having looked deeper into that prayer and reading about it, there is no shame in asking for blessings. That is, if they are in line with God's will.

Letting God use your life to reach others. Wow, the trials a person would go through and the tests to be faced, to see if we even measure up to front line material. Scary, huh? You bet. That's where faith comes in. If you have faith the size of a mustard seed, then stand on it. Because we are in a time where we have to live by faith not by sight.

The circle has come around in a full rotation. I have enjoyed the time of walking that I've done here on earth, but as the months have passed and the pain increases, a wheelchair has become part of my life again. I am limited to the time I can stand thanks to the demons called "pain" that are biting at my ankles. It feels like someone cut my left ankle and then forces me to stand on it without letting it heal, thus, stumbling over the demons every day. Sometimes catching myself before falling, then there are other times when I meet the wall or floor with my face.

Yet, Satan watches to see my reaction and waits for my next move. God also watches and at the same time, the One I call Father, reaches out and lifts me to a level I could not get to on my own. Remembering the first time He touched me. The way he spoke to my heart, the gentle way he whispered into my ear. The tone of voice that built me up and enveloped me in the love he said belongs to me by right.

The inheritance is ours, if we wish to belong. Adopted into a family so big we have yet to see all of them. The names we know. We know them by actions of the heart. God has a loving heart that He wants us all to have. He has blessings we are deserving of but are afraid to ask for. Let's not play 'cat and mouse' just be direct.

Daily we are blessed. Daily we are tested. Daily we pass and fail. We never know when or where the blessings will pop out. That's when our faith is stretched. The longer we stretch it, the stronger it becomes.

Want a second chance at something? Ask for it. Walk by faith. Listen for his voice and lean on him and not your own understanding. Look with eyes that are not your own and you just may see a blessing coming your way.

As humans, we tend to want to give up or give in when we see the end of something. As we grow and trust, we see death, not as an ending, but rather a beginning. In order for there to be life, there has to be death. We die and we are re-born everyday. Recognizing the death of flesh and birth of spirit isn't hard to do if we're on the right road.

Will the road we're on lead us to Him? Will we dance to the tune of a harp? Or will we dance to the echo of our screams on the dance floor of eternal flames?

"Oh, that You would bless me indeed..."

THE NEXT PHASE
Chapter Forty-Nine

Wow, to see things come full circle, hmmm. To be in a wheelchair again after so many years of walking, is a surprise but not entirely unexpected. Life is full of changes and this is going to be an adjustment, not only for me, but also for everyone who knows me.

The first day at work with the wheelchair, was a tidal wave of mixed reactions to my new mobility. Yet, the true test was my reaction to everyone else's reactions. Most of all, my co-workers were cool with the wheelchair; others however, were shocked and saddened. To them I said, "Don't be sad. These wheels are not the end of my life, but rather the beginning of a new phase. I only have to feel the pain in my legs when I stand in the check stand. The rest of my time at work will be in this chair and off my feet."

With each positive encounter I had, one man's name came to mind, Jason Schlegel. Jason helped a lady forget she was in a chair by dancing with her. The people who know me soon forgot about the wheels and saw only me. I'm not sure how many people feel about me, but I'm sure they see that I'm not giving into this handicap. I'm stepping into the next phase.

A day or so later, I got a call from a friend's mother. Her son, Rod, went into the hospital to have a cancerous thyroid removed.

When I got to see Rod after the surgery he was struggling with the scar and the new phase in his life. As he tried to hide the scar and go about his daily chores, I watched and told him, "I'm not going to help you until you ask." I smiled.

Rod replied, "That's exactly what Jesus would say."

We laughed as he again tried to hide the scar on his throat. "Rod, you don't need to hide that scar from me. That scar is not you, but it is a part of you. I have scars that I want to hide, but there are times when I can't. You would say the same thing to me."

When Christ was taken from the cross, the holes and scars from the nails remained. He took those nails and died so that the world could have life. Christ showed the holes to doubting Thomas to prove that He came back from the dead.

Many of us have scars, some physical and some

emotional. Some scars may be seen and others not seen. All of the scars will heal, most will remain.

As Rod has to learn to live with his scar, I have to learn to live with my new wheel chair. It has opened my eyes to the possibility that my job may end if adjustments cannot be made at work and the pain doesn't stop. I have jumped heart-long into my writing, that I may get it off the ground.

Two books of poetry are waiting to be printed. Trying to raise the $1500.00 per book is slow and has been placed into prayer. (Getting one book to the printers by the end of September, will be putting it available by Christmas.) As I pray about those two books, I am diligently working on a book of inspirational stories called HIS ONLY TEAR. Any help that can be given in getting these projects off the ground will be appreciated.

The Lord doesn't close a door without opening another. Pills may replace a thyroid and wheels may replace legs, but life goes on and dreams will be reached. Things happen for a reason and they happen in His timing.

A FATHER'S LOVE

Chapter Fifty

I held you in my arms on the day of your birth. I watched every gesture. I heard every sound. My heart leaped with joy for your life was fresh and new. The world would know how proud I was to be your father.

It has been a while since we've talked. It gets tough to communicate at times, but I really miss those times when you'd tell me what was on your mind. I'd just like to listen to you, even if there's nothing I can do to help. I'm here for you. Do you know that?

I couldn't imagine life without you and yet you won't look at me or call me by name. We've drifted apart. Life has placed a gap between us. For years, I've wanted to bridge that gap and draw closer to you, but the more I try, the further you get. Why is that?

Things happen for a reason, that I understand. We all have emotions tied up inside of us that hurt when we let them out. It's okay to cry. Cry all you want. Just let me know how you are doing and what you're thinking. I'd love to get to know you better...if I knew where you were.

There was a time when I thought we'd be inseparable. Oh, how I longed for that to happen. There's nothing stronger than a praying family. Be prepared, when a family begins to pray together, the enemy will attack. The enemy hates unity and will stop at nothing to tear down the foundation of prayer in a family. Daily we are tested. Sometimes we pass and sometimes we fail, that's only humanistic behavior. We don't have to give in or give up. We just move on to the next test.

Daily I pray for you. I ask you, will you forgive me if I've failed you in any way? I've really wanted to keep in touch. I've tried talking with you, but the lines of communication have been cut between us. I'm still here for you. I've never moved. I'm still where I was when we last talked. You can find me if you want to. I know you have a lot of questions and need a lot of answers. Forgive me, if I cry for you. You may think I have no right to cry when it comes to you, but I do. When it comes to you, my emotions swell up to overflowing and I just need to let it out.

When your life began, you and I bonded within our

214

hearts. I felt that tight knit connection. I miss that. Over the years, the tightness has come loose, but I feel the bond is still there. There are always two sides to every story. You have only heard one of them. One day, I'll tell you my side.

You may never have called me Daddy or even known me as him, but I was there at your birth and we talked when you were a small child. Your heart knows and it feels what I know and feel in my heart. I may not be the daddy figure in your life, but I will always be your father.

As your father, I will pray for you. I will keep my eyes open for you. If it happens that we should never meet until we have both passed on, I will tell you then, and show you, that a gap can be bridged. You will see with your own eyes and know in your heart, that a father's love never dies.

ASKING FOR FORGIVENESS
Chapter Fifty-One

For most of my life, I've been driven by the desire to write. Writing anything I could that would get readers in touch with the truth. There are times when I get "Writer's Block" and cannot write to save my life.

As I think of new writing projects and titles that I'd like to do, I see the dust gather on passed efforts to be "one day, published." I then begin to cry and wonder why I let life's situations keep me from doing what it is God wants me to do. Then the very next thought is, "it's okay for me to use the money for the books to live off of. The books will be printed when the right time comes." Within a month or so, book sales slowed down. The wind had been taken out of my sail and the momentum diminished.

September 03, 2001

During lunch at work, I prayed, *Dear God, please forgive me for not doing what you asked me to do with the funds given to me for the sales of my books. I know I need to trust you in every area of my life. I admit that I have failed in that area. I ask you, Father, to forgive me. Will you let me have another chance to make it right? If given the chance, I will do what you want me to do.* Forgiveness brings about release.

September 05, 2001

I was eager for my shift at Albertson's to come to an end. My vacation and my 33rd birthday were on the sixth. I looked at the rows of people lined up to get their food.

This is unbelievable. I've only been here thirty minutes and we're already swamped with customers. We're short courtesy-clerks and checkers. This isn't the way I want to remember my last day here before I start my vacation.

Moments later, a gentleman with a friendly smile wished me a "happy birthday" with a firm handshake. In that handshake was a folded piece of paper. When the rush slowed, I stepped out of the check stand and unfolded that paper. I fell over when I saw what it was. A check for $500.00! (The exact amount needed when sending in the manuscript for one of my books.)

Humanistic behavior took over. I began to make mental

list of things to do with the money. Pay off credit cards? Rent? Buy groceries? I bought a money order for $300 during a break.

I stuffed the rest of the cash into my pocket. After work that night, I set out to buy groceries.

"Where'd you get the money for food?" My wife asked when I arrived home.

"A customer blessed us with $500.00. I bought the food, but I'm not sure what to do with the rest of the money."

"Pay some of the rent."

After that, I began losing sleep. It was hard to go through my day and not think about what had happened. How I had let my Father in heaven down by not following through with what I was told to do.

Father, again I come before you and ask for forgiveness. I failed you once more with the funds. I'm sorry.

September 10, 2001

I stopped by the post office to check the mail. A 'yellow slip' was there. A package was waiting for me. I sat in the car outside of the post office. A message in a birthday card read, "just be the person God wants you to be.' – your biggest fan, J9.

How sweet. I thought as I set the card aside and reached for the package. Inside was a Christian Writer's Guide. With that was another card. Folded inside the second card was a check for $500.00. *WOW! Another check. I know exactly where this is going.*

I drove to the bank, got a cashier's check for the full amount and went home to call the publishers. The final touchups were made to the manuscript for the re-print of THE HEART OF A MAN: A Collection of Poetry, Book One.

September 11, 2001

That manuscript was on its way to Morris Publishing. Once again I've placed my life and my work in the hands of Jesus. I trust that the final funds and the book will be done by Christmas 2001. Thank God for forgiveness!

I also learned of the tragedies that struck this nation. As we pull together, we will pray for the strength and unity. This world is now in His hands.

Author: Lacy Johnson
September 11, 2001

I'm not a priest who can lead you in a prayer.
I'm not a victim who can say I was there.
I'm not a rescue worker who can say I tried.
I'm simply an American, who felt the pain and cried.

I'm not the President who can say Justice I will find.
I'm not a survivor who will never have peace of mind.
I'm not a doctor who can say I've done my best.
I'm simply an American who will cry when they are laid to rest.

I'm not on the ambulance crew who can say I saved a life.
I'm not a family member who lost a husband or wife.
I'm not a news reporter who was there for the world to see.
I'm simply an American who felt the shock and terror rip
through me.

I'm, not an airplane pilot that died at the hands of a madman.
I'm not a loved one who will never fully understand.

I'm not a building that had to crumble and fall.
I'm simply an American who has felt it all.

In memory of all the victims and their family members. May God bless America!!!

ONE MORE DAY: UNITED WE STAND

Chapter Fifty-Three

Early that morning the phone rang.

"World War Three is here. Take cover and be ready." Said the voice on the other end.

"I'm in bed right now and my head is covered. What are you talking about Bro?"

"The world is coming to an end. A plane was high-jacked and plowed into the World trade Center buildings in New York."

"If this is true, man, this is a wake up call. Are you ready for that?"

Click. Dial tone.

I jumped out of bed, ran to the living room and turned on the television. WOW! A second plane crashed into the other building in New York.

Little did I know how much this attack was going to affect me, I watched in shock and denial as the newscast plastered on the airwaves.

In the last few days, as I drive home from work, I find myself brushing away tears brought on by a song on the radio. I knew one thing, we all prayed for ONE MORE DAY.

This nation, once a bunch of strangers who never dared to give someone a second glance, has become a family brought together by terrorists to show love and comfort for our fellow Americans. I tear up at the simple thought. Here I sit in my home wondering, *what can I do?*

I haven't the money. Nor can I give blood, but when my time comes to give, I will rise to the occasion and do my level best to see it through. My pains are felt, but are minor. My struggles, though hard, are but shadows compared to the monstrous pains and struggles this nation as a unit is feeling.

I wrote a story called A FATHER'S LOVE on September 1st, 2001. That story was a tough one to write and in the wake of the horrors we witnessed on the 11th, that story now has DOUBLE meaning for me, as I know that our Father in heaven will watch over us and protect us as we are left behind to regain our strength. At the same time, He has welcomed home several of His children as they passed on in the tumbling towers in New York, Washington DC and Pennsylvania.

WHAT CAN I DO?
I watched in disbelief
I listened intently
Hugging my loved ones
Thanking God for the blessings I have received
Now I cry and dream in tears
As though I'm drowning in helplessness
Wanting to do more than my circumstances allow
What can I do
All that I try to do
Isn't nearly enough
Others dig to free strangers
They now think of as family
I sit wanting to do more
I'm not on television
Not even am I on the radio
Women, children and men all the same
Pray for strength and closure
Answers yet to come
Faith stepping up
All this man can do is pray
I long to lend a hand
In more ways than I am
United I want to stand
But on bended knee
I pray for those lost
And those fighting to protect this land

Hatred is killing but love is healing. Wounds are deep and will hurt for a long time to come, but life at some point has to go on. I stop daily and pray and want to see others smile through the pain. I am but one man in a sea of lives placed on this earth by God. My life may not be much to myself or to some stranger on the street, but those lives lost in the midst of tragedy have touched me even here at home. Can we stop asking why one man would have another without question? Helping others brings about blessings for all involved. Life is a blessing in a white box with red ribbon tied around it.

A soul harvest is upon us. Eyes have been opened. A voice has been heard. We listen closely now, but will we continue to listen even after the terrorists are brought to justice?

Towers may lay in ruin and lives may have been taken, but from the darkness, life will emerge. Hatred may have reared it's ugly head and tried to kill a nation, but as a nation, we shall stand in unity unlike any other, a love stronger than an attack.

This is not the end, nor is it the beginning, rather just a segment of a story. For life as we once knew it, will forever be changed. Will we look at people the way we once did or will we as Americans see people through God's loving eyes?

He cried a tear that day I'm sure. I'm also sure it won't be His last.

WHEN SILENCE IS DEAFENING
Chapter Fifty-Four

The terrorists had a secret they didn't tell us. Many people kissed and hugged in the early hours that day. Not knowing that it was the last time. Were the words "I love you" said that day?

Life went on as usual, until…BAM! Time froze and life took a quick turn. Lives were lost and souls went home.

Seasons change when the time has come. We cannot control what happens, we can only sit back and watch as life unfolds. Gold, red, brown, and orange fall to the ground without a care. Scorching summer days are gone and autumn is slipping fast as well. Soon the blanket of winter will be here, but few will feel warmth.

There are reasons for everything. Some things just happen while others give reason for their cause.

In all things there is joy, happiness, sorrow and pain. Through every season we gather strength. Getting stronger because of what we go through, but unable to see the big picture unless removed from it.

This world has gone to war and who knows when it will end. We will all feel the pain and deal with it in our own way. There will always be people out there who want to take the easy road in life while controlling those around them. They want to take the credit without lending a hand, or quick to point fingers without seeing the problem through to the end. The decisions we make today, we will have to sleep with tonight. Are we ready for that? In the last month or so, this country has become united. United we stand and divided we fall. Some people say they stand for what is right, yet tear down the support group around them. In every area of our lives, we are a team. A team is only as strong as its weakest link. If the strongest link has to pull twice the load, he too will break down. We shouldn't want to shred the foundation that makes us strong. One person cannot do it all.

Followers must be taught to lead before taking that position, yet if those who teach will not take the time to teach, they should be prepared to take the blame and not shove it on to the next in line. We ALL have to do our part to stay strong or the wrong person may get hurt. We need to work for the greater good of everyone around us. There isn't one person 'better' than another. If you want to lead and have your own 'team', you better be willing to jump in with them to fight the battle, otherwise the very fabric that we call 'teamwork' will disintegrate from within.

From the nation to our workplace and even in our homes, don't break down what needs to be built up. Don't yell if wrong moves are made, if right procedures haven't been taught. Don't try to take the lead if you're going to be the first to bail out. Don't shift blame on your responsibility.

If a war is being fought by order of mouth, yet the one giving orders is hiding from the fight, the backlash will burn in the end.

THAT BOY
Chapter Fifty-Five

During my Freshman year at Marble Falls High School in Marble Falls, Texas I saw a fellow classmate, a boy that no one wanted to know. Have you ever met a kid like that? He was a boy that the 'rich kids' called a 'waste of yearbook space'.

That boy was different. His hair was long. He walked differently. He wasn't at all like everyone else. He was teased by most of the school. Even few of the teachers teased him in a roundabout way. He wore hand-me-down clothes, yet never complained of anything. He was always alone, no friends to speak of. Kids saw him in class and kidded with him, but behind his back they made fun of him. No one knew his mother or father since they were rarely seen around town. That boy stayed to himself and never spoke unless spoken to. Students liked him that way. 'Less noise in the hall' except for when he walked or ran for class. Then he sounded like an elephant in the hallways. That boy couldn't use the bathroom without being harassed by other boys. The other kids called him gay. At seventeen, that boy wasn't sure himself what he wanted or what he felt. Aside from being teased all the time, his record at school was okay. He worked hard and tried to do his best.

That boy went in for surgery during the year and 'friends' came out of the woodwork only because it got them out of class early so they could take turns pushing that boy down the hall to the next class.

Now, that boy wasn't rich like most of the kids he knew. Heck there were kids in his class whose parents owned half the town. The girls he wanted to date, laughed in his face when he asked them out. The boys he admired teased him till they fell out of their chairs.

That boy had spent most of his Junior High years with these other kids, but their attitude towards him was the same then too.

However, in 1984, there was this one boy "Brett", who in a fleeting moment took the time to say 'HI' to that 'ugly duckling' of a kid. That boy was taken aback by the generosity of a fellow student's reaching out, but at the same time, just said 'Hi' as he walked past.

Later that year, it was made known to the boy that "Brett" killed himself. The reasoning for the death is still unclear to several and maybe not even remembered by most. I can't help but think what may have happened to "Brett" that day he met that boy if that boy had known Christ. One simple handshake could have saved a kid's life. But no, that boy, he knew of God but he knew nothing of Jesus.

His birth father was no where to be found, his mother worked all the time and her boyfriend drank from sun up until sunset. That boy lived in a condemned home across from a dog pound. He barely saw the folks he lived with and seldom went to church. If there were any Christians in that school, he didn't know it.

In August 1986, that boy's mother took deathly ill with cancer. He went to school like nothing had changed but when the word got out, he was called to the office from every period. Once there, he found gifts from anonymous persons. Although this was a touching thing to do, what no one realized is that that boy was going to see another Christmas, but his mother wasn't. What were they doing to help ease her pain? A new watch or boom box wasn't going to pay the bill or make her hurt any less. As shy as he was, he took the gifts and went back to class.

Two weeks before his mother's death, his birth father showed up in town. The boy was happy to see that his dad was there for him, but that wasn't the case. His dad was there to remove that boy from his mother's home in the time that she

231

needed him most. That boy told his father to return where he came from and began praying for strength as he watched his father leave town once again. Soon after his mother's death, that boy left Marble Falls.

That boy has never stopped praying for his family and others and has since come to know Jesus stronger than ever. I don't know if he has ever seen any of his old schoolmates, except for one. They didn't talk then, but they talk on occasion now.

What would you do if you met a 'That Boy' or a 'Brett'?

That boy still isn't much in the world's eyes these days, but in the eyes of his daughter, he's the best daddy ever. And you know whom he has to thank for that? Jesus Christ. Thank you God for the love you shower upon your children.